ATLANTIC
Barnegat
Toms River
Forked River
Rt. 40
Lakehurst
Naval Station
Old Road
P   L
Creature Comfort
Fort Dix
Mt. Misery
Fire Tower
Lebanon State Forest
Philadelphia
New
N
E
W
S

OCEAN
Barnegat Light
Cedar Beach C.G. Station
Bay
LIBRARY
Shack of the Plotters
U.S. 9
Barnegat
Manahawken
ountains"
AINS
Rt.s 40
N
S
Tuckerton
Cedar Bridge
Swamp
Wading River
Chatsworth
Je r sey
A Birdseye Map of Ted's Country
Edward Shenton

SHADOW IN THE PINES

SHADOW IN THE PINES

by STEPHEN W. MEADER

Illustrated by EDWARD SHENTON

SOUTHERN SKIES

ISBN 978-1-931177-32-0 cloth
ISBN 978-1-931177-33-7 paperback

SOUTHERN SKIES

LITTLE ROCK, ARKANSAS

www.southernskies.com

SHADOW IN THE PINES

1

WHERE THE SUN CAME THROUGH openings in the overhanging trees, the sand of the narrow road glared white and dazzling. Ted felt the warm, clean grains of it sifting between his bare toes and dragged his feet slowly, reveling in the sensation. It was only mid-April, but hot as June.

He swung his books in their long strap from his right shoulder to his left and turned off on a deer path that offered a short-cut through the woods. It was Friday afternoon and school was over till after Spring Vacation. The boy whistled contentedly at the thought. Two weeks to cruise as he liked in the Pines! He'd have another try at that old trout in the lower pool. The arbutus would be flowering early in this heat, and he'd make some money selling it. Then he could visit his friend, the fire warden, and maybe put in a day or two gathering peat-moss. Besides, he still had some exploring to do up toward Fort Dix, where the new reservation fence ran through the woods. With so many alluring projects running through his mind, he hardly knew what to plan first.

The bushy pitch pines and scrub oaks shut out the sunlight now, and Ted's faded khaki shirt and old dungarees blended with the soft, gray-green shadows of the spring woods. He stopped whistling and went on silent feet, hoping to surprise a deer or a fox.

Small, bright-feathered birds hopped and twittered among the laurel leaves and a pair of cardinals called cheerfully to each other in the tree-tops ahead. But though the boy's keen eyes searched the brush on both sides of the trail, the first four-footed beast he saw was his own dog. Tramp was a black-and-tan mongrel shepherd. He had figured it was about time for his master to come home from school and was trotting leisurely up the path to meet him.

Ted threw down his books and caught the big dog's paws in his hands as Tramp leaped up in greeting. They stood almost the same height, for the boy was small for his fifteen years. He dodged a moist flick of the dog's affectionate tongue and picked up the books again.

"You heel, now, Tramp," he ordered sternly. "Heel an' go quiet, or you'll scare every critter in the woods."

It was a good two miles from the tarred road, where the school-bus let Ted off, to the home clearing. He had covered nearly three-quarters of the distance now, and was starting down through the tangled cedar thicket that grew in the swampy ground along the creek. It was hot enough for a swim, he thought, if there had been more water. As it was, weeks of dry weather had lowered the level of the dark, slow-moving stream and there was a sticky margin of muck along either side. Back in February the boy had taken nearly fifty prime musk-rats in his traps along the creek-bank. Now the root-sheltered mouths of their burrows were left high and dry above the water line.

He followed the twists and turns of the path toward the fallen log that served him as a bridge. It was just as he was about to cross that he caught sight of the man on the opposite bank.

Without a sound, Ted ducked behind a laurel bush and pulled the dog down beside him. Strangers were rare indeed in his out-of-the-way corner of the woods, and the boy thought this one needed investigation. He was certainly acting queerly.

From what could be seen of him, the man across the creek was young—not more than twenty-four or twenty-five. His head was bare and the sun glinted on his curly, red-brown hair. He was dressed in what looked like well-worn hunting clothes and had a small knapsack strapped on his shoulders. Ted knew the things he was holding up to his eyes were field-glasses because Joe Lucas, the fire warden, had a pair. Through them the stranger seemed to be intently studying a clump of sassafras a few yards away.

After a moment he let the glasses swing on their strap and pulled a notebook out of his pocket. There was a look of satisfaction on his face as he wrote something in the book with a pencil. Then, without turning, he spoke.

"Hi, there!" he called. "Thanks for keeping quiet, but you can come out now."

Ted thought for a moment that there must be another man, somewhere out of sight. But the stranger looked straight toward him and grinned. "I got a glimpse of you back there in the cedars," he explained. "It was just luck, though. I didn't even hear a stick snap."

Somewhat shamefaced, the boy got up and crossed the log bridge. Tramp, bristling and growling, followed at his heels.

"Shut up, you," Ted told the dog. "Don't mind him, Mister. He just isn't used to having folks around."

"No," said the stranger, "I suppose he doesn't see many, this deep in the Pines. You live 'round here?"

"Yonder," Ted pointed eastward. "I'm going that way now."

"Mind if I come along? My name's Bill Gates. What's yours?"

"Ted Winslow."

The young man held out a sun-browned hand and, after a second's hesitation, Ted shook it.

"I reckon you wonder what I was doing just now," Gates chuckled. "I'm a sort of amateur naturalist. Like to study birds, among other things. I don't know whether you've noticed, but the warblers are migrating early this year. That little blue fellow I was watching was a parula—they don't usually come through here till a week or two later."

They were following the path that led up through thick pine woods, away from the creek. Ted went first, keeping a sharp watch among the branches overhead. He had never paid much attention to the smaller birds, but if they were all the stranger wanted, he thought he could show him plenty of them.

"There," he whispered, stopping and pointing ahead. "Is that one?"

Gates looked over his shoulder. "No," he laughed, "that's no warbler. That's a chickadee. Wait—hear him call? *Chick-a-dee-dee-dee.* That's where he gets his name."

"Oh, sure," said Ted, flushing a little. "I'd have known what 'twas if I'd listened first."

They had gone less than a hundred yards when he halted again. In a thicket of laurel bushes to the left of the path, he had seen a small yellow-headed, olive green bird flitting. He half-lifted his hand and at that moment a dreamy little song rippled back to them.

"Good work!" Gates whispered. "That's a real find—a black-throated green warbler. Watch a minute and see if you can see him from the front. He's got a white belly and a handsome black bib across his throat."

They waited, motionless, for a full minute before the restless little bird hopped into full view.

"Yeah—I see it!" Ted breathed. "You mean there aren't many like that around here?"

"Oh, for a day or two there may be hundreds, but this is the first one I've sighted this year. Warblers, you see, are great travelers. Most of them breed and nest way up in Canada or the northern edge of the United States—some as far north as Hudson's Bay and Labrador. They raise their babies up there, and in the fall, when the young ones are strong enough to fly, away they go to warmer countries."

"Gosh!" said Ted. "You wouldn't think they could fly that far on such small wings."

"Well, they take it pretty easy and stop to eat every few miles. Their food is bugs—little moths and flies and other insects. That's why they don't come through Jersey until it's warm enough for the bugs to hatch. That black-throated green we just saw must have started months ago. He and his mate spent the winter clear down in the Central American jungles."

Ted was beginning to get interested. "Say," he remarked, "you sure know a lot about birds. Do you do this for fun, or do you make a living out of it?"

Bill Gates laughed. "It's just a hobby of mine. I take a few days off in the spring and see if I can beat my record. The migrations are early this year and I missed the first wave, but I've got forty or fifty species in my notebook since yesterday."

They were at the edge of the clearing now. Off to the right an old cranberry bog stretched away between flanking arms of woodland. Ahead of them, across a sandy-looking patch of plowed ground, was a square, two-story frame house, its shingles weathered gray. Behind it stood a ramshackle barn. There were lilac bushes in the front yard, and a rambler rose bush climbed a trellis by the door.

"You live here with your folks?" asked the young man.

"Just my grandpap," Ted answered. "He's all the folks I've got left. He'll be glad to see you. Sometimes he gets lonesome for a visitor to talk to."

The boy led the way past the front door and around to the back, where sounds of activity came from the kitchen. Half a dozen hens of assorted colors were clucking and scratching in the sand by the steps.

"Gramps!" Ted called. "We've got company."

In the doorway appeared a small, wiry man of sixty-five or more. He had a great shock of upstanding white hair, and his seamed face was burned by wind and sun to the color of old leather. A pair of very bright blue eyes peered from beneath his bushy eyebrows.

"Find yourself a shady spot an' set, stranger," the old man nodded. "I've got supper to get, an' Ted, here, has to do a couple o' chores. We'd take it kindly if you'd stay the night."

"Thanks," said Gates. "I'll accept your hospitality if it won't be too much trouble, sir. Mind if I go along with Ted? Maybe I can be some help with those chores."

The old man chuckled. "You don't look to me like a feller that has done much farm work, but you do whatever you've a mind."

As he turned back into the kitchen it could be seen that he stumped along on a wooden leg.

Bill Gates mentioned the fact as he and Ted went toward the barn. "Too bad your grandfather's crippled," he said. "How did he lose his leg?"

"Crippled!" the boy snorted. "I bet you never saw a fellow his age that got around any spryer than Grandpap. He's had that peg for more'n forty years. Got a bad wound at San Juan Hill with the Rough Riders, and they had to take his leg off. He's sort o' proud of it."

"I should say he had a right to be! Was your father a soldier, too?"

"Yep. He served in the A.E.F. An' my great-grandpappy Winslow was in a Jersey volunteer regiment. Got wounded at Antietam. I reckon our family's got Army in its blood."

Ted fed the chickens, collected four brown eggs from the nests, and threw down a forkful of hay for Doc, the old horse. Dotty, the brown and white spotted cow, was out at grass in the little pasture beyond the barn. She wouldn't be brought in and milked till after supper, the boy explained.

He and his guest each picked up an armful of sticks from the pile by the chopping-block and carried them in to fill the wood-box. There was a delicious smell of frying ham and eggs coming from the stove, and the old man was stumping about, setting the table.

" 'Tisn't as if we had women-folks to do for us," he told Gates. "But we get enough vittles to keep us going, an' manage to get along without the frills."

Ted brought a jug of milk from the cool-cellar and they sat down to their meal. Grandpa Winslow was a good cook. There were fluffy hot biscuits and a huckleberry pie made from fruit he had canned himself.

There was plenty of talk that evening, both at the supper-table and in the comfortable front sitting-room after the milking was done. The bird-man was a good listener. He showed a lively interest in local history and asked a good many questions about the scattered people of the Pines.

"You seem to have quite a few deer-hunting camps in the woods around here," he remarked. "I suppose they're more or less of a nuisance to folks who live here the year 'round."

"Well, it's only for a few days in deer season," the old man replied. "The city fellers come in droves then, an' they go banging around like a thunderstorm. It's much as we can do to get us a buck for winter meat. But they don't stay long, an' it's rare to see 'em around any other time o' year. Yes, there's quite a mess o' deer camps. Three I know of betwixt here an' Mount Misery."

"Queer names the old settlers gave places in the Pines," Gates laughed. "Long-a-coming and Apple Pie Hill and Ong's Hat and Double Trouble and Mount Misery. What do they call this section?"

"Used to be known as Nine-Mile," the old woodsman chuckled. "Nine mile from nowhere, I guess. My wife changed the name when we cleared here an' built this house. She was a good, church-going woman an' she named it 'Creature Comfort.'

That's what we still call the place."

They talked about some of the old "ghost towns" of the Pines, the early furnaces and forges where bog iron had been turned into cannon balls, stoves and farm tools back in Revolutionary times.

Grandpa Winslow settled back in his comfortable rocker and filled his pipe. "Towns? Yes, they were towns, all right," he said. "I've heard old-timers tell about 'em when I was a boy. Places where there'd be as many as sixty or eighty houses—stores, an' taverns, an' even churches. Maybe four-five hundred folks would live there. Some of 'em dug ore out o' the bogs. Some worked at the furnace, or the bar-iron forge, or the foundry. Some drove teams, hauling iron to market. An' there was always a mess o' choppers an' charcoal-burners in the woods for miles around. It took plenty o' charcoal to keep a big furnace in blast.

"Some o' the old iron-masters had mighty fancy places, I can tell you. Big, fine houses, with ball-rooms an' servants' quarters. What became of 'em? Well, 'long about a hundred years ago the coal an' iron mines in Pennsylvania got started, an' the price of iron went down. By that time the bog-ore was pretty well used up. Folks down here couldn't make their furnaces pay. I guess the old people just died off an' the young ones drifted away. The roofs fell in, after a while, an' brush grew up in the dooryards, an' forest fires maybe finished the job."

Gates nodded. "It sort of gives you the creeps, doesn't it?" he said. "I've seen some of those old places. All you can find now is a house chimney standing by itself in the pines, or part of a furnace wall, or a rusty old iron casting. The woods have swallowed up everything else. It makes you think this part of the country is bound to be wild, and nothing men try to do will change it."

The old man struck a match to re-light his pipe. "That's the gospel truth," he agreed. "Now you take this Fort Dix reservation. Reckon the Gov'-ment's spending millions o' dollars there, to build what they think is a bang-up, last-word military camp—a reg'lar city for soldiers that'll stand there forever. I can see it, though, forty years from now.

Some committee in Washington'll forget to repair the fences, an' the woods'll come creeping back, soft an' easy. An' some day young Ted, here, he'll be exploring 'round an' come onto a busted-down shack with an old Piney like me a-setting on the doorsill —just deer an' turkey-buzzards for his neighbors. 'What's this place?' Ted'll ask him. An' the old feller'll spit terbaccer an' say, 'This? Why, this here's Fort Dix!' "

Ted, huddled down in a corner to listen, happened to look at the stranger just then. In the light of the oil lamp his mouth had a grim look and his brows drew down in a hard line. It was as if a shadow crossed his face. He rose abruptly and went over to the open window.

"Yes," he spoke without laughter. "Fort Dix could disappear. And it could happen in a lot less time than forty years."

Then he turned to the light once more. "Sorry, Mr. Winslow," he grinned apologetically. "I was talking to myself. Must be about bed-time, isn't it? Where do you want me to sleep?"

The old man sprang up and went to a shelf in the kitchen, where two or three well-polished oil lamps stood in a row. He lighted one and handed it to his guest.

"We got a spare room," he announced proudly. "Don't get to use it often, but it's kept ready. You'll find it right there at the head o' the stairs. Good night, an' I trust you'll sleep comfortable."

2

TED WAS AWAKE BEFORE DAYLIGHT. IT wasn't time to get up yet and he lay there in his cot under the eaves, listening to the first sleepy chirping of birds. The sound swelled into a full chorus as the east grew gray, but the boy only half heard it. His mind was busy trying to recapture the exact words and the tone of Bill Gates' remark the night before. Something about that moment had startled Ted and set him wondering.

All his patriotic feelings were tied up with Fort

Dix—the huge, sprawling Army cantonment that had become a neighbor almost overnight. When his grandfather had joked about its disappearance, Gates hadn't seemed to think it was funny. "It could happen in a lot less time than forty years"—that was what he said. But what did he mean?

The Winslows rarely saw a newspaper, but they had an old battery radio that kept them aware of what went on in the outside world. And at school there had been plenty of talk about the war and America's preparations for defense. "Fifth columnist" was a phrase familiar enough to Ted. He knew that enemy agents were actual people, not merely fiction characters. And he knew that they were smart enough not to go around looking and acting like comic strip spies.

The stranger had a disarming friendliness that had made Ted like him from the first. He still wanted to like him—but now an unhappy suspicion had crept into his mind.

He pulled his clothes on and went out to do the morning chores before anyone else was up. When he returned to the house their guest was already at the breakfast table, chatting with Grandpa Winslow over the flapjacks and coffee. Ted barely answered the young man's cheerful "Good morning." He ate with his eyes on his plate and took no part in the conversation.

"Teddy," said Grandpa, when the meal was finished, "Mr. Gates wants you to go 'long with him a piece. You can show him where the old Shamong road cuts through, this side o' Muffin-Top Hill. What ails you, anyhow, boy? Must have got out the wrong side o' bed, I reckon. Wake up, now, an' show you know your manners."

Before they set out, Ted got himself an old market-basket from the shed. "Thought I'd go down to that place I found an' get some arbutus before it's done blooming," he explained to his grandfather. "If you won't need me for anything I'll likely be gone all day."

"I'll make out," the old man told him. "Watch out you don't pull up the roots, or there won't be any flowers another year. Here—you better take along a snack o' lunch."

He sprinkled several flapjacks with brown sugar and rolled them up in a piece of paper. With a couple of apples out of the bin in the cool-cellar, Ted was well provisioned.

The sun was up but the air was still cool when he and Gates left the clearing. There seemed to be birds everywhere. They had been walking only a few minutes when the naturalist pulled out his notebook and jotted down a fresh name. This time it was a Maryland yellow-throat that he had seen.

"A chap like you ought to learn something about birds," he told Ted. "Living right here in the Pines you've got a great chance to see them. Tell you what I'll do. I've got a handy bird-book with colored pictures, back in Philadelphia. Next time I come through this way I'll bring it to you."

Ted's delight couldn't be held in. "Gee!" he gulped. "Thanks. I'd sure like to have it. When do you think you'll come again?"

"Oh, it shouldn't be long. I expect to be hanging around here quite a bit this summer."

Then the boy remembered. That miserable doubt of Gates' motives came back to bother him, and he shut up like a clam.

They followed the sandy ruts of the old road three miles to the westward and came to a similar woods track that crossed it at an angle.

"Let's see, now," said Gates. "This ought to be the old Shamong road down to Chatsworth."

"That's right," the boy replied. "You could go straight ahead an' come out on the new road, but this way's shorter when you're afoot."

"And where's Muffin-Top Hill from here? That's where the fire warden's tower is, isn't it?"

"Yes," said Ted. "You can't see it through the woods, 'cause the hill is just a little rise o' ground. But you can see a long way from the top o' the tower."

"Well, so long, son," Gates smiled. "I'll pay you another visit before long, and I won't forget that book."

Ted watched him stride off down the sandy track. When he was out of sight, the boy turned back and traveled something over half a mile before he reached a deer path meandering off to the south-ward.

That morning he had left Tramp tied up by the barn. Now, as he followed the winding path through pine and scrub oak thickets, he wished he had brought the dog to keep him company. Blue jays squabbled noisily in the pine tops and a song sparrow was making spring music in a clump of blackjack oak. After a time the trail dipped toward lower ground and Ted's bare feet squelched in the damp moss of a swamp. Kneeling, he began to dig with his hands among the coarse grasses. He found what he wanted—a deep layer of matted peat-moss.

The boy filled the bottom of his basket with the moist, clinging stuff. It made an ideal sponge for keeping flowers fresh. Ted knew families in the Pines who made a living gathering peat-moss for the city florists.

He was still on his knees by the path when a tiny noise made him look up. There, not a dozen yards away, stood a red doe and her small, spotted fawn.

Ted kept perfectly still. The deer were watching him, but he knew that as long as he did not move, their curiosity would keep them there. At last he could hold his breath no longer. As he drew air into his lungs the doe snorted and turned in a graceful leap that carried her several yards into the brush. The fawn followed as if he had been tied to her apron strings. It was a buck fawn, Ted was sure, because there was a double line of white along its back. A single line would have meant the baby was a doe.

The swamp was noisy with the piping of young frogs and the chirp of birds among the cedars. It was long but not very wide—and Ted crossed it in a few minutes. Actually he did not think of the place as a swamp at all but as a "cripple." In the language of the Pines the word meant a boggy woodland along a half-stagnant stream.

A little way beyond he came to the old railroad track, stretching lonesomely away into the wilderness to the northeast. He crossed it and entered a belt of woods where the undergrowth was fairly clear and white sand lay underneath the dead leaves.

As the sun rose higher the summer-like heat returned, and the boy could feel it baking his shoulders through the cotton of his shirt. The time was early for snakes, but he knew this was rattlesnake weather. He picked up a stout stick and walked carefully, watching the ground ahead of him. Rattlers didn't frighten Ted. Like most youngsters in the Pines he went barefoot almost from frost to frost. He had seen plenty of snakes and killed more than one, but as his grandfather used to say, "Only a born fool or a city feller'd ever let himself get bit by a rattlesnake."

Hiking steadily southward for another hour, the boy came at last to the edge of the woods. The big oaks and pines ended as cleanly as if they had been cut off. Yet no ax had ever cleared the vast stretch of rolling moor that lay beyond. He had reached the borders of that strange region known as the "Plains."

Ted had never heard of the learned treatises written about the origin of the Plains, or the arguments among scientific men that had grown heated without ever arriving at a definite conclusion. All he knew was that in a total area of some forty square miles no tree ever grew much higher than a man's head. There were pines and oaks there, leather-leaf and turkey beard and sand myrtle—nearly all the kinds of vegetation found in the neighboring forest. But the trees were stunted and dwarfed to pygmy size. When a buck was moving through that growth you could see his antlers a good half mile away over the tree-tops. In the far distance, even now, he could make out the flash of sun on speeding cars where the state highway cut across the Plains on its straight route to Manahawkin and the shore.

The boy stood for a while looking out over the sun-swept, gray-green expanse. It always gave him a feeling of exhilaration when he came to this place. It was so big and so lonely under the empty sky, where a solitary hawk wheeled high in the blue.

But much as he enjoyed the sight, Ted was no dreamer. He had a job to do that morning. Here at the edge of the Plains, where nobody ever came, was the finest arbutus patch in all South Jersey. He had discovered it the year before on one of his long rambles with Tramp. Half shaded under the little oak trees, the tell-tale leaves and shy pink-and-white flowers were in sight from where he stood.

As he knelt beside the nearest cluster the fragrance of the blossoms made him bend his head, sniffing hungrily. It was the sweetest smell in the world, he thought—all the freshness of springtime in a flower tinier than his finger-tip.

He picked with skillful hands, lifting away the brown leaves and twigs under which the blossoms hid. The stems were like small creepers, wandering from a parent root. Carefully he nipped off each one three or four inches below the bloom. It wasn't stems that people bought, anyway. It was flowers, and they'd never see any nicer ones than these.

Ted didn't have a watch, but from the sun he judged it was nearly noon when at last the basket was piled high with arbutus. He sat down in a shady place and ate his lunch. There was no water near but the winter-kept apples still had enough juice in them to quench his thirst. When he had tossed away the last core he reached in his pocket for a neatly rolled ball of string and began tying the blossoms into bunches. There were twenty of these tucked down in the damp moss on the basket-bottom when he finished.

Looking south across the Plains to the Manahawkin road, he was tempted to try his luck with the flowers there. But he knew what rough walking it was through that low-growing brush, and he would be an extra two miles from home. Besides, it was the Sunday drivers who made the best customers. He decided to wait till next day and peddle his blooms along the Lakehurst highway, nearer the clearing.

Ted followed a different trail on the way back. Up to the westward, above the "cripple" where he had dug the peat-moss, there was an old dam and a shaded pool. In spite of the heat, the boy ran the last hundred yards, and as soon as he had set down his basket he began snatching off his clothes.

Even at high water, the pool was hardly deep

enough for diving, and now he knew it would be foolish to try. But at least he could get wet. The brown cedar water was cool to his skin. He swam quickly across, then rolled on his back and floated lazily, staring up through the leafy roof above. A red squirrel on the bough of a sweet gum chattered at him with angry jerks of his small body.

When he had had his fill of swimming, Ted crawled out on the clean sand of the bank and let the sun dry him off. There was a three-inch pine lizard sitting on top of his clothes when he went to dress. He made a grab for it, but the little blue-gray fellow was far too quick for his fingers. It darted around the nearest tree trunk and disappeared in a split second.

Ted loafed on the way home. He tried to see how quietly he could thread his way among the thickets and pine clumps. Now that his eyes had been opened, it was amazing to find how many different kinds of birds there were in that sunny wilderness. If only he had the promised book he was sure he could have found out the names of a dozen small, bright-hued warblers. Studied at close range they glittered like tiny jewels, vivid with blue, green, yellow and black.

The feel of the hurrying spring was in the air. Buds were swelling on the bushes along the trail. Maples growing along the water showed red blooms against the soft blue of the sky. It wouldn't be long before the laurel blossoms and the wild azaleas and the small white bells of the blueberries filled the Barrens with color and scent.

It was about four in the afternoon when he neared the sand road that the fire warden used in going to Muffin-Top Hill. He was about to cross it when he heard the sound of an approaching car. It was a smooth-running motor—not the noisy old woods-buggy that Joe Lucas, the warden, drove.

Ted drew back behind a screen of leaves to let it pass, and in a moment he saw a dusty, black convertible whipping the close-growing brush as it sped along in the sandy ruts. Then the boy nearly dropped his basket in surprise. For in the quick glimpse he got of the driver he recognized the stranger who had spent the night at Creature Comfort.

Gates had not seen him, he was sure. He waited till the dust had settled and the car was out of sight, then turned and followed it. There was something more than queer going on, he decided, when a man who pretended to be hiking afoot through the Pine Barrens suddenly turned up in a car.

All his doubts about the young naturalist returned more persistently than ever. On that particular road, he knew there was only one place the man could be going, and that was to Muffin-Top, half a mile ahead.

Ted moved fast, his toughened feet padding in the sand. In a few minutes he came in sight of the tower and saw the black car standing under the pines close by. He left the road then and went cautiously through the woods. Soon he was near enough to get a good view of the railed platform at the top of the 75-foot structure. His friend, Joe Lucas, was nowhere in sight.

But there was a man up there—a bareheaded man

with red hair. Even at that distance, Ted had no difficulty in identifying Gates. He was leaning his elbows on the railing and looking off to the northwest through a pair of field-glasses.

The boy waited, still half hopeful that the stranger was merely looking around at the scenery. But the glasses never wavered. They were pointed straight at the nearest corner of the Fort Dix reservation, three miles away across the woods.

3

THERE WAS NO SUN OVER THE BAR-
rens the next morning. A low fog had rolled in from
the sea and covered the pine belt with a gray blanket. Ted thought it might mean rain, but his grandfather sniffed the air and shook his head.

"No such luck, I'm 'fraid," he sighed. "Wind's
still in the south, and this is just a dry fog. She'll
burn off by the middle o' the forenoon. It's a good
thing there's no danger o' frost. I could flood the
bog once with the water that's back o' the dam, but

once is about all."

In addition to his Spanish War pension, Mr. Winslow earned a few dollars a month by acting as caretaker for the old Atkins cranberry bog which lay next to his property. In spring, when the cranberry plants were coming into blossom, a killing frost might do untold damage if the bog could not be flooded at a moment's notice.

Ted understood the old man's anxiety, but he wasn't exactly sorry that the day turned out fair. He knew a hot Sunday afternoon in April would bring swarms of motorists on the main roads to the seashore. With that fact in mind, he ate a hasty lunch and set out northward, carrying his basket of arbutus. Once more he tied Tramp up at home, for the dog wasn't used to highways or speeding cars.

On the four-mile journey through the woods, Ted had plenty of time to think about Bill Gates and his strange visit to the fire tower. He tried over and over again to find a satisfactory explanation for what he had seen the afternoon before.

Possibly the convertible was a borrowed car. Or

it might be that Gates had driven it down from the city and left it somewhere near the main road while he hiked through the woods. But he hadn't been driving like a man who was simply going to look at a view. He was in a hurry. And even from a distance Ted had felt the urgent tenseness of his pose, as he stood up there on the tower, studying the military reservation.

As far as the boy could see, all the evidence pointed one way. He had said nothing to his grandfather because he was sure the old man would laugh at his suspicions. But there ought to be something he could do about it.

He resolved to talk to Joe Lucas, the fire warden, as soon as he got the chance. Joe, who had been on that job for thirty years, had seen a lot of queer things happen. In any case he would be interested in knowing that a stranger had used his observation post.

Ted came out of the pines at the edge of the highway. Looking up and down the long, straight ribbon of concrete he could see at least a score of cars, all heading shoreward. Hopefully he set down his basket and held out a bouquet of the sweet-scented blooms.

"Arbutus!" he yelled. "Twenty-five cents a bunch!"

But the cars whipped past him like the wind, and the roar of their speed smothered his voice. He kept on trying for several minutes without catching the attention of a single motorist.

Hot, hoarse and discouraged, Ted sat down at last. Somehow he had to figure out a different plan of attack. He didn't know much about driving automobiles, but he had seen enough of them to realize that it would take a long distance to stop one going fifty miles an hour. No matter how attractive his flowers might look to lady occupants of a car, he couldn't expect the driver to turn around in traffic and come back for them.

Half a mile to the westward the highway came around a fairly sharp curve, and was crossed there by a gravel road. Perhaps the cars would be moving more slowly at that point. Anyhow he had nothing to lose by trying.

As he trudged along, the boy saw two cars pull off the road ahead and swing out on the grass, in the shade of a clump of trees. Then several people got out, carrying picnic baskets and rugs. By the time Ted drew near they were all seated on the ground, laughing and talking as they opened wax-paper parcels of food. He resisted the temptation to go up to them at once and try to make a sale. Common sense told him that hungry people were likely to be poor customers. Quietly he sat down on the root of a big oak, a little way off, and settled himself to wait.

There were four couples in the party. Young married folks, he judged them to be—full of fun and having a thoroughly good time.

When the sandwiches were gone and second helpings of cake and fruit were being passed, Ted got up and walked slowly toward the group. He had timed his approach well. Full of food, the picnickers were lolling back with every sign of contentment.

A few kidding remarks were addressed to him by

the men, but he only grinned and held out a bunch of pink blossoms. "Got some nice, fresh arbutus, right out o' the woods," he said. "Reckon you won't find better any place. An' it's only a quarter a bunch."

"Ooh!" cried one of the girls, clapping her hands. "I love it! Please—may I sniff!"

She buried her nose in the cluster. "Tom," she said, "I've simply got to have some for that green bowl on the table at home."

Her husband laughed and reached in his pocket. "I'll take two," he told the boy. "How about the rest of you? I used to pick arbutus when I was a kid, but I never saw any that could touch this."

Before he left the roadside party Ted had sold six bunches, and there was $1.50 jingling comfortably in his pocket. He went on up the highway to the curve and stationed himself just beyond the cross-road, holding a bouquet of blossoms in either hand.

As he had hoped, there was a definite slow-down in the pace of the cars as they approached the turn.

Every few minutes a woman passenger would notice the flowers Ted was holding and the driver would put on the brakes, swerving out on the broad gravel shoulder. One by one the bunches of arbutus came out of the basket and the weight of silver in the boy's pocket increased. When the last of the flowers were sold and the earnings counted, he felt proud of his week-end's work. He had an even $5.00. Adding it to his trapping profits he would have a sizeable fund to use for next winter's clothes and shoes.

It was only about three o'clock and for the rest of the afternoon he could do anything he liked. If he followed the highway toward Mount Misery he'd have time to stop at Ace Pittman's place and see the snakes. And from there he could cut over through the woods to the tower on Muffin-Top, where he hoped to find his friend, the fire warden.

Half an hour's walking brought him to a highway bridge over a single-track railroad line that drowsed sleepily in the sun. He scrambled down the embankment and went a short distance up the track.

Back in a clump of trees was an old frame house, weather-blackened by the years.

Ted knocked at a door on the creeper-covered porch and waited, but there was no answer. In a cage near the door a red squirrel leaped gracefully back and forth, pausing occasionally to stare at the visitor with beady black eyes. A soft rustling sound came from another wire-fronted box. Stooping to look in, Ted saw three good-sized rattlers moving sluggishly in a tangle of gray, brown and black coils. Close by stood more cages, holding pine lizards, bright-hued coral snakes and a huge king snake.

Everybody in that part of the Barrens knew Asa Pittman. He had been catching reptiles for nearly forty years, and many of the big city zoos were his regular customers. Ted took a last look at the pets and set off southward into the pines. Before he had gone far, the rough path he was following plunged down into a cedar swamp. Deep in the shadows a dark little stream twisted among the roots. The boy waded across and emerged in a brush-grown glade, sheltered by a curving, wooded ridge. He was pushing through the bushes hunting for the path when a man spoke a few yards off.

"Mind yer foot," said a mild voice. "That's a big 'un. More'n twelve rattles, I'd judge."

Ted looked hastily at the ground and saw a rattle-snake as thick as his arm sliding through the dead leaves. He jumped back involuntarily. At the same moment a raw-boned figure stepped from behind a scrub-oak clump and a long arm reached out with a forked stick, deftly pinning the snake to the ground. The man moved without hurry. One of his hands slipped along the writhing body and seized the rattler just behind its ugly head.

"Yessir," he remarked, holding the captive up at arm's length, "he's got fourteen or fifteen rattles, an' he'll measure better'n five foot long."

With that, he dropped the snake into a stout canvas sack slung from his shoulder and greeted Ted with a twisted grin.

"G-gee, Ace!" the boy stammered. "It's a good thing you spoke when you did."

Pittman's blue eyes twinkled in his craggy,

weather-seamed face. "Shucks," he said, "ye wouldn't ha' got bit. Pays to look where ye step, though. This holler's plumb full o' snakes. Some calls it the rattlesnake den, 'cause they hole up in here in the winter."

"Well," Ted replied, "you can bet I'll be careful next time I take this path. I'm glad I saw you catch that one. You sure do a neat job!"

"I ought to," the backwoodsman laughed. "Had plenty o' practice at it. Where ye bound, sonny?"

"Figured I'd stop by Muffin-Top on the way home," the boy explained. "If I can find my way through, that is."

"'Tain't difficult," Asa told him. "Jest over the hill, there, ye'll strike a deer path that'll take ye within sight o' the tower."

Ted bade him good-by and started on. For the next mile he watched the ground ahead of him with a good deal of care. Any boy who had been as close as he had to stepping on a big rattler was bound to be snake-conscious. Probably if he had not been looking about so sharply he would have missed the faint glint of metal that caught his attention. It was buried in the leaves, a yard to the left of the narrow deer track.

Stooping, the boy picked up a pair of short, heavy pliers. They were well-made and had a bright finish. Back of the strong jaws there was a sharp-edged slot for cutting wire. How they came to be out there in the deep woods was more than Ted could understand.

He still had the pliers in his pocket when he came out of the pines at the foot of the fire tower. Joe Lucas' ancient car was parked under the trees and Ted could see the stout form of the warden on the observation platform.

"Hi, Joe!" he yelled. "Anybody up there with you?"

Lucas' face appeared over the railing like a red moon. "Hi, Teddy," the warden shouted. "Nope. I'm all by my lonesome. Come on up."

The youngster went up the series of steep steel ladders like a squirrel. At the top, Lucas was holding the trap door open for him. He was a big, stocky man, ruddy-faced from long days in the open.

"Ain't seen you in over a month," he grinned. "How you been, an' how's your gran'pappy?"

"Both of us fine," Ted replied. "I've been up to Route 40 with a mess of arbutus. Sold out an' came back this way to talk something over with you. Do you know a city fellow named Bill Gates?"

Lucas nodded. "He's been comin' down here in the spring for a couple o' years. Matter o' fact he stopped by my place yesterday."

"Did you know he came up here in the tower?"

"Sure. He asked me if 'twas all right. Why?"

Ted was somewhat taken aback. "Well," he hesitated, "maybe I've figured him out wrong—only it struck me as mighty queer."

He went on to tell the warden about Gates' strange remark when his grandfather had mentioned Fort Dix. "He never told us he had a car, either," said Ted. "When I saw him driving so fast through the woods I hustled over here, an' sure enough he was in the tower, with his glasses aimed right at the Fort."

Lucas reached over a huge paw and tousled the boy's hair. "You been worryin' too much," he grinned. "Hearin' spy-stories on the radio, I reckon. This Gates looks to me like one o' the nicest young chaps I ever met. Knows a lot about birds an' animals, too. Might be his doin's look funny to Pineys like us, but all city folks are queer in the head—'specially these scientist fellers."

Ted was only half convinced, but he could think of no further arguments. He turned to the circular table in the middle of the platform. Under a sheet of glass there was a map of the whole fire district. With the location of the tower as its center, the circle was divided into sixty-four segments, like slim slices of pie. Ted knew that when Joe Lucas saw the smoke of a forest fire he could sight along those lines and tell where it was within a mile or less. Then he could call the deputy warden nearest the spot and send a crew to fight the fire. There was a telephone in a wooden box beside the warden's chair.

"Where's our place on the map?" the boy asked. "Oh, I see it. 'Atkins' Bog,' it's marked. An' it's in section 18."

He found the "18" mark, cut in the tower railing and borrowed the warden's binoculars to look in that direction. But the rolling tops of the woods stretched away eastward without a visible break.

"Can't see the house or the clearing," he said. "Anyhow, I hope you'll never spot a fire in 18."

He was getting ready to leave when he remembered the pliers in his trousers pocket. "Say," he remarked, pulling them forth, "did you drop these, Joe?"

Lucas examined his find curiously. "Nice pair," he observed. "Don't know's I ever saw any just like 'em. No, they ain't mine, Teddy. Where'd you find 'em?"

"Over in the woods, a quarter of a mile north," said Ted. "There's no rust on 'em, so they can't have been lying there long."

Lucas turned the pliers over and looked more closely at the trade-mark stamped on the side. "Hm," he grunted. "It's a furrin name. 'K-R-E-U-Z-E-R-F-A-B-R-I-K' is what it looks like. Ain't that last part German for 'factory'? I picked up a few words o' the lingo when my outfit was stationed at Coblenz, after the war, but I've forgot most of it."

Ted stared at the pliers with a new interest. "Gee," he said, "you don't suppose"—but he checked himself for fear of being laughed at. "Well, as long as they aren't yours, I guess they must belong to me, huh? Finders, keepers." And he slipped the shiny things back into his pocket.

"If anybody asks you about 'em, let me know," he added as he started down the ladder.

"Okay," chuckled the warden. "So long, Ted— and don't go dreamin' about spies tonight!"

4

THE PUZZLE OF THE PLIERS OCCUPIED
Ted's thoughts most of the way home. It would be
strange if even a single person, outside of himself
and the fire warden, had so much as set foot in that
stretch of woods since Christmas. A few hunters
might have passed that way during the deer season,
in early December, but the condition of the steel
made it seem impossible that the pliers could have
lain in the woods through four months of winter
weather.

There was only one man he could think of who might have dropped them more recently—Bill Gates. And what would he be doing with foreign-made tools? In spite of Joe Lucas' reassuring words, the incident added fresh fuel to the boy's suspicions.

Back at Creature Comfort, he did the evening chores and told his grandfather about his successful arbutus sales and his meeting with Asa Pittman. "That was a mighty big snake—a reg'lar whopper," he concluded. "But you ought to see how easy Ace handled him! He sure knows snakes an' varmints."

"Yep," the old man chuckled. "An' he knows 'em nat'ral, without book-learning. Now that young fellow, Gates, he's studied Natur' in books. He stopped here this afternoon, by the way."

Ted pricked up his ears. "That right?" he said. "What was he after?"

"Oh, he was asking a lot o' questions—mostly about what he calls the 'Lost Forge.' Wanted to know if I'd ever heard old-timers speak of it. I told him it used to be a sort o' fairy story when I was a youngster. There was an old Piney, name o'

Cudjaw Tewks, came into Chatsworth one day for provisions. Stopped by Buzby's store an' claimed he'd found an abandoned iron works nobody knew about. Cudjaw must ha' taken two or three shots o' Jersey lightning, for he swore up an' down he'd been in the iron-master's house an' it was still standing— handsome as a king's palace. But drunk as he was, he wouldn't tell how he got there. An' nobody more'n half believed him anyway, 'cause he was known to be crazy as a coot."

"Didn't anyone ever try to find the place?" Ted asked.

"Oh, sure. There was a spell there, back around 1890, when we kids spent a lot o' time looking for it. Used to pack a blanket-roll on our backs an' stay in the woods three or four days at a time. But old Cudjaw never told, an' he was drowned in the Wading River a couple o' years after that. I don't know where Gates got a hold o' the tale, but he's got an idea there's some truth in it. Anyhow, he wanted to know about Cudjaw's habits—where he fished an' hunted an' so on. There wasn't much I could tell him, for the old fellow was sort of a wandering hermit—always wilder'n a fox."

"Gee!" Ted mused. "Wouldn't that be something, if you could find it? What do you think, Gramps? Could a forge an' a house be lost, like that?"

"Pshaw! I wouldn't know. It's hard to believe, but I've no doubt there's parts o' these woods that haven't seen a human for fifty years. Don't you go sky-hooting off to look for it tomorrow, though. It'll be Monday—that's wash-day. Long as you're not in school, you better be on hand to help."

Ted knew it bothered his grandfather's rheumatic joints to lean over a washboard, so he cheerfully scrubbed out the clothes next morning and hung them to dry. The summer-like heat continued and there wasn't so much as a cloud in the sky.

By ten o'clock the boy had finished and asked Grandpa Winslow's permission to take the rest of the day off. "I'm not going to hunt for the Lost Forge," he grinned. "Just thought I'd hike across and see what the Army's doing with this new part o' the Fort Dix reservation. I'll do some ironing to-night, if you want."

The old man offered no objection, and Ted was soon on his way, a parcel of bread, butter and ham for rations tied to his belt. He crossed Route 40, went on across the Barrens to the old Lakehurst road, passed a long stretch of cranberry bogs and cultivated blueberry bushes, and plunged into the woods again. After a while he came in sight of what looked like a narrow clearing, and he knew he must be getting close.

The Fort Dix fence, when he reached it, was something of a disappointment. No sentries with fixed bayonets challenged his approach. Only a pair of jays peered at him raucously from a sour gum tree. He could see that a sort of rough fire-break had been made through the pine and scrub-oak growth, leaving a clutter of brush and fresh-cut stumps. The fence ran along the middle of this forty-foot cleared area. It was built of heavy wire, fastened to steel posts, and he judged it must be seven or eight feet high. At the top the posts bent outward and held several strands of ugly-looking barbed wire. It wouldn't be easy to climb over, the boy thought, unless the intruder had wire cutters.

On the other side there seemed to be nothing but a continuation of the wilderness. No barracks were visible—no huge airfield, or hangars, or drill-ground. Ted knew that the older part of the camp was six or seven miles away, at Wrightstown, but he had hoped the Government was using the new section for something more thrilling than this. He went westward along the fence till he came to a spring where a tiny stream of water trickled down a mossy bank. As it was already past noon he decided this would be as good a place to eat as any, and lying down in the shade of a blackjack oak he opened his lunch.

It was while he was enjoying the last of the ham sandwiches that he heard a rustle of leaves behind him. He turned quickly and shielded his face as a big, black, hairy shape launched itself at him.

"Doggone you, Tramp!" he scolded, trying to avoid the animal's fervent caress. "How'd you get here? I left you tied!"

A length of frayed rope, attached to the dog's collar, showed what had happened. He had gnawed loose and trailed his master all those miles from home.

"Well, now you're here," said Ted, "I s'pose you might as well eat." He gave Tramp the remnant of his bread and ham and rolled over to drink from the spring.

As he raised his head and wiped his dripping mouth, the dog crept close to him and began growling, deep in his throat. Ted put a hand on his collar. Up along the fire-break, two hundred yards away, he saw a man approaching slowly. For a moment he did not recognize the figure. Then he caught the glint of sun on red-brown hair and knew he was looking at Bill Gates.

The young naturalist was coming along beside the fence, stopping every few paces to examine the posts and wire. He still had the field-glasses slung around his neck but he no longer wore his knapsack. What he was doing now certainly had no connection with birds. In fact, at that moment, Ted saw a small, bright-colored warbler flit across the clearing not a dozen yards from Gates' head without attracting his attention.

Ted lay still and kept the dog quiet. He wanted to find out if the man had merely been lucky on their first encounter or if his eyes were actually as sharp as they seemed.

When he was about thirty yards away, Gates stooped to check a strand of wire with his fingers. Then, as he straightened up, he swung toward the boy. "Hi, Teddy," he said without smiling. "You and Tramp seem to turn up in a lot of places."

Ted would hardly have known the gay young man who had said good-by to him two days before. There was a hard, tired look around Gates' mouth, and a furrow between his eyes. He came over to the spring, drank thirstily and sat down on the moss. "I'm tired," he yawned. "Things have happened fast since I saw you. I got five hours' sleep last night and none the night before."

He shot a look at Ted and grinned as he saw the

boy's uncomprehending stare.

"I guess it's about time I took off the false whiskers," he said. "No reason why you shouldn't be quite a help to me. Who did you think I was?"

Ted felt his face grow hot, and the suddenness of the question left him tongue-tied.

"I could tell," laughed Gates. "You were the only one who didn't accept me at face value, as a harmless city man with a weakness for birds."

He got up and scanned the woods behind them with a long, searching glance. "Just as well not to have any eavesdroppers around," he explained. "Well, Ted, you can rest easy. I'm not an enemy spy. As a matter of fact my right name *is* Bill Gates, and I *do* like to take bird trips. But I'm a lieutenant in the U. S. Army, too. Army Intelligence. My job is to see that nothing happens to Fort Dix."

A long sigh escaped Ted's lips. "Gee!" he whispered.

"I wouldn't tell you this if I didn't know I could trust you to keep your mouth shut," Gates continued soberly. "Nobody else, not even your fine old soldier of a grandfather, must suspect what I'm doing."

He passed his hand across his face in a gesture of weariness.

"Somewhere down here in the Pines," he went on, "there's a secret radio station. We haven't been able to spot it from the air, or get an exact location from our receiving sets. But it doesn't move around. It always seems to come from one place. They've been sending in code—a tough code, too—but Washington has deciphered it at last. I got news Saturday that these people, whoever they are, have been planning some kind of a surprise move aimed at Fort Dix."

"Is that why you were up in the tower?" asked Ted.

"Yes. So it *was* you in the woods when I drove by? Didn't have time to say hello then. There was something I wanted to see from the top of the tower.

"All that night I was cruising around in my car, and listening on the receiving set. They were sending messages every hour or two, but I couldn't seem to get it any clearer in one place than another. The dot-dash code they use is bad enough, and even after it's been deciphered the messages are hard to understand. They're all in riddles."

He hesitated, looking at Ted as if he wanted to be sure of something. Then he reached in his breast pocket and pulled out a crumpled paper.

"Here's one I caught early Sunday morning," he said with a frown. "I can't make much out of it, but decoded and translated it goes like this: 'Now proceeding with plan four, to be ready G. Most comfortable here but need salad, soup, cake. Leave them E, hour 26, where venison crosses iron. Saw three hawks today, one red fox.'

"We don't know, of course, just what 'plan four' is. 'G' and 'E' are days, and 'salad,' 'soup' and 'cake' are code names for different kinds of supplies they want brought to them. Anything in the rest of it strike you as interesting?"

Ted thought for a minute. "Well," he said, "if they're any place in the Barrens, they'd never see a red fox. All we have 'round here is gray foxes."

Gates nodded approvingly. "Right! It proves they're strangers in this neighborhood—and of course they didn't mean a fox at all. I think I can explain that one. They meant *me*." He grinned and pointed to his auburn hair. "And the 'three hawks' were observation planes we had scouting over the Pines, Saturday. Anything else?"

"Well, yes," Ted answered. " 'Venison'—that's deer meat. The part about 'where venison crosses iron' made me think o' places I've seen where a deer path goes down into a swamp an' there's tracks in the red bog iron along the edge o' the water."

Gates' lips pursed in a silent whistle. "I wonder," he murmured. "Maybe you've got something there. You know I've searched every hunting camp and checked up on every charcoal-burner's shack and farmhouse within twenty miles, and haven't run across anything that could be their hang-out. So I figure they must be in a place that's completely hid-den—lost, if you like. That's why I asked your grandfather about the Lost Forge. I believe that's the sort of spot they've found—somewhere deep in a swamp where nobody would ever think of going. Maybe they outsmarted themselves with that crack about 'venison' and 'iron.' "

"I never put much stock in the Lost Forge," Ted told him. "Stands to reason somebody'd know about it."

"Well, we've got the county authorities in Mount Holly digging through the old records. Practically all the old forges and iron works have been located years ago, and there are deeds and legal papers to prove where they stood. But they've found one deed, dated 1797, that seems to be kind of a mystery. It's in the name of a man called Jared Classon and it mentions a 'tract of 9,000 acres for an iron furnace on the Hoquadunk Stream, beginning one mile south of Elder's Branch.' Ever hear either of those names?"

Ted shook his head. "They must ha' been called something else for a long time," he said. "I'll talk to Grandpap some more. He might recollect hearing old folks tell about 'em."

The lieutenant stretched his arms and sprang up. "I've taken enough time off," he said. "We have an idea somebody's been getting through the fence, so I'm checking the wire pretty thoroughly."

That word "wire" touched off Ted's memory. He pulled the pliers out of his pocket.

"I found these in the woods," he said. "They were beside a deer path, over north o' the fire tower on Muffin-Top."

Gates examined the pliers carefully, and a gleam came into his eyes. "That's it!" he exclaimed, half to himself. "That's the first break! You really found something, Ted. Mind if I take them along? Headquarters ought to have a look at these."

He rubbed his chin thoughtfully. "I've got a hunch you can be quite a help to me," he said. "If you learn anything that seems important and you want to reach me in a hurry, get to the nearest telephone and call this number."

He repeated the figures slowly and had Ted say them back to him. "Don't write it down anywhere. Just fix it in your memory," he told the boy. "When you've got the connection, ask for J-21. That's me. And if I'm not there, they'll get the message to me. So long now, youngster, and good luck!"

Ted watched the red-haired young man move off along the fire-break, then called his dog and started homeward. He was happy to discover how wrong he had been about Gates. But more than that he was full of a sense of pride and importance over the trust the young lieutenant had placed in him. What a day! He vowed to himself that he would find the spies' hiding place before vacation ended if he had to hike a hundred miles!

5

IT WAS LATE AFTERNOON WHEN TED
got back to Creature Comfort. His grandfather was
nowhere in sight, but Doc, the horse, was still in
his stall, so he knew the old man could not have
gone far. He went about his evening chores, filling
the wood-box, gathering the eggs and feeding the
chickens. The heat, which had been oppressive all
day, hung heavy over the clearing even though the
sun was near the horizon.

Ted sat down on the back steps and thought

about some of the things Gates had told him. In a minute or two he saw his grandfather's wiry figure stumping along the path from the bog. The old soldier pulled out a blue bandanna and wiped his face when he reached the yard.

"Blamed if I ever lived through a spring like this," he growled. "Worse'n you'd expect in August. Well's mighty low, too. If it don't come on to rain this week we'll be hauling water for the stock. Well, Teddy, did you find Fort Dix still there?"

The boy was itching to tell somebody his news, but he remembered Gates' warning and merely grinned. "Yep," he said. "All serene. Say, Gramps, did you ever hear tell of a creek called 'Hoquadunk'?"

The old man turned at the kitchen door and shot a keen glance at him. "Hm," he grunted. "Run across that Gates feller, did you? He asked me the same question. Nope, never heard of it. Used to be an old Injun with a name something like that, though. Lived down Atsion way. Mebbe the stream had an Injun name an' the white folks changed it, but that'd be long before I was born."

When supper was over and the evening milking was done, Ted came in to find his grandfather filling his pipe. The boy had been waiting for this moment. During the busy hours of the day the old soldier was apt to be short and crusty in his speech, but once he relaxed after work he liked to talk.

"I was trying to remember, Gramps," Ted began casually. "Didn't you mention knowing some folks named Elder, once?"

"Elder? Elder—why, sure, I might have. Used to be some of 'em 'round when I was a youngster. Le's see, there was Kenny Elder from over Injun Mills way. Sort o' weak-minded, he was. Didn't have all his buttons. An' I recollect some Elders that lived down along the Mullica, near Green Bank. Any special one you wanted to know about?"

"Well, no." Ted shook his head. "I heard there used to be a creek called Elder's Branch, but I reckon it was nearer here than either o' those places."

"Doesn't sound familiar to me," the old man replied. "Still, there's little streams all through the Pines an' they have different names, different times."

That night in bed, Ted lay awake for the better part of an hour, puzzling over the spies' code message and the clues it might contain. He had not written it down, but he remembered it almost word for word. He wondered how the supplies they asked for would be delivered. Few cars or trucks entered the maze of ancient, brush-grown sand roads that wandered in a spidery network through hundreds of square miles of the New Jersey Pine Barrens. Yet a horse and wagon would be slower and more likely to arouse suspicion. Gates, Ted was fairly sure, had already taken steps to have the main roads watched.

The boy's thoughts skipped to the code words about "venison" and "iron." If there had been anything in his hunch, there was something he could do. He resolved that the very next day he would start exploring south and east in the wild country beyond Woodmansie. It was the only section within ten miles that might hide a forgotten swamp or cripple where bog iron would be found. With a plan of action in his mind, he quickly fell asleep.

It was a little cooler when he woke at dawn. He dressed quickly and hurried out to do the milking. The sun was just rising as he came back from the barn, full pail in hand. No cloud was in the sky, and the dry, parching air still came lazily from the south. For a moment he stood there, sniffing uneasily. There was a tang in the breeze—a faintly pungent smell of wood-smoke. The disk of the sun was red as it cleared the tree-tops, and that, for people who lived in the Pines, was another evil sign. Somewhere a long way to the southward a forest fire was burning.

Grandpa Winslow had smelled the smoke, too. He watched Ted wrap a paper of lunch when the dishes were done and frowned a little. "Wouldn't go too fur today, if I was you," he remarked. "Woods are dry as tinder. No telling when some fool's going to toss a match out of his car an' start a reg'lar old hum-dinger of a fire."

"I'll keep watch," Ted answered. "You'll see me back here if the smoke gets thick."

He snapped his fingers for Tramp to follow him and crossed the clearing to the old sand road that led eastward. There were warblers by the score, hopping and singing among the buds and new leaves. The boy tried to identify the ones Bill Gates had shown him. He wondered when his friend would find time to bring him the promised bird-book.

In the more open patches, where the morning sun streamed down through the trees, creamy white spikes of turkey-beard rose above the low growth of leatherleaf and huckleberry. Occasionally Ted caught a glimpse of tiny, shy, pink flowers on a shrub that he recognized as sand myrtle. Tramp trotted busily ahead, scouting both sides of the road for the faint, exciting scent of squirrel or cottontail, raccoon or gray fox.

Where the ruts turned north, two miles from the clearing, Ted left it and swung to his right into the woods. There was no trail here—nothing but the crisscross pattern of deer paths—and the boy went by the sun, keeping it straight before him as he headed southeast.

He had been moving through the woods for perhaps an hour when his bare toe stubbed against something hard among the matted leaves and creepers. The injury wasn't serious but it made him angry, and he hopped on one foot, holding the bruised toe in his hand, while he looked for the cause of the trouble. It had felt like a stone but he knew there was no surface stone in that part of the Barrens. When he found it at last, and scraped the leaves away, the object turned out to be a piece of baked clay, pinkish brown in color. Its surface was perfectly flat and its unbroken edge was square. He knew at once it must be a fragment of a larger slab, made by men's hands. This piece was some eight or ten inches across and a little over two inches thick.

Curious, Ted turned it over. On the side that had been downward there were scraps of earth and leaf-mold, and a small black spider that scuttled off in haste. But what caught the boy's eye was a series of letters indented in the flat surface. He bent closer, scraping away the dirt with a bit of stick. On one line was the complete word "LIES," and below it the letters "DER"—apparently the ending of another word, the first part of which had been broken off.

Ted knew then that he had found a piece of one of the old terra cotta grave markers, baked from native clay. He had heard of them but it was the first he had ever seen. Lacking any kind of stone except iron ore, and wanting to use something more lasting than wood, a few of the earlier inhabitants of the Pines had used such slabs to mark their burial places.

Tramp saw that his master was interested. He sniffed at the fragment, then began nosing among the leaves, a few feet away. Ted encouraged him. "Good boy, Tramp!" he said. "Come on—we'll find the rest."

Between them it was not long before they had uncovered four more, smaller fragments and one large piece that must have formed the lower half of the stone. But fitting them together was a more difficult job. There were still a number of scraps missing when the boy knelt over the assembled slab and began to decipher the faint lettering. As nearly as he could make it out, the inscription read:

```
. . RE LIES
. . REMIAH . LDER
Bo . . . . rch 8th, 1816
Died Sep . . . ber . . d, 1831
Sayfe from this Sadd
Worlds Alarms
Resteth in his
Maykers Arms
```

Ted didn't laugh at the quaint spelling. He felt a swift compassion for this youngster—just about his own age—who had died in the wilderness so long ago, and been so utterly forgotten. The first name with its missing letters must have been Jeremiah. Probably they called him "Jerry." The last name was more puzzling. There seemed to be room for only one letter before the "L," and it would have to be a vowel. Ted's mouth formed whispered

combinations. Older? Alder? More likely an "E"—
Elder.

He sprang suddenly erect, staring down at the
broken marker with mounting excitement. "Gosh,
Tramp!" he murmured. "D'you reckon it could be?
'Elder's Branch'—what we've got to do now is find
the nearest stream o' water!"

With a woodsman's instinct, the boy went slowly
southward, studying the contour of the ground. In
that rough, brush-covered country there were no real
hills or valleys. Only a native of the Barrens would
have noticed the gradual slope of the land that
turned Ted toward the east after a few minutes'
walking. Soon he came to a little clump of cedar
trees and his feet sank in cushiony peat-moss. Those
signs meant boggy ground close by. He moved on
for another fifty yards and his heart began to beat
faster. Right in front of him he saw the glint of
water through the brush. It was only three or four
feet across but it was a stream. It wound sluggishly,
like a dark snake, half hidden among the twisted
cedars and tangled huckleberry thickets.

For a moment Ted could not be sure which way the water was flowing. He dropped a dry leaf on the surface but the light breeze from the south moved it back toward his feet. Then he cut a chip of wood and placed it in the middle of the stream. It lay too low in the water to be affected by the wind. Very slowly the chip began to move to the right, and the boy had his answer.

He followed the course of the stream southwestward, fighting his way through scrub oak and cedar and thorny holly. His progress was slow because he was afraid he would lose the little brook if he took short cuts. So he stayed within sight of the water, even when it seemed to double back on itself in its aimless wanderings.

The sun was high now and midsummer heat blanketed the April woods. Occasionally Ted stopped to sniff the sultry wind, but the taint of smoke was no stronger than it had been in the early morning. Doggedly the boy plodded on for another hour. He had only a vague idea where he was, but he was sure that in all his previous roaming he had never been even close to this particular area. He had covered miles without crossing anything that looked like a trail, much less a wood-road. There were a few big, weather-grayed stumps in the swamp to prove men had been here once to cut the cedar, but it must have been long ago.

At last he came to a boggy spot where the brush seemed to grow thicker in front of him. It was a discouraging prospect and he stopped to wipe his sweaty, briar-scratched face with his bandanna. Tramp had trotted on along the boggy margin of the stream. As Ted started on he heard a splash. He thought the dog must have jumped into the rivulet to cool off, but when he pushed through the bushes, a moment later, he saw the familiar black head moving across a wide expanse of water. Elder's Branch— if that was what he was following—had suddenly found its outlet in a larger stream.

Ted whistled, but the dog paid no attention to him. He was in hot pursuit of a brood of fluffy mallard ducklings, all hurrying for the reeds on the opposite bank. Just as Tramp was lunging forward through the water to seize the nearest baby, the mother duck gave an anguished squawk and hurled herself with flapping wings straight at the dog's head. He stopped swimming, snapped once or twice in a futile effort to ward off those buffeting pinions, and turned in ignominious retreat. Ted was still laughing when Tramp dragged himself ashore.

"You old fool," he chuckled, "served you mighty well right—picking on those cute little fellers!"

The dog gave him a reproachful look, shook the water out of his thick coat, and ambled off into the woods, thoroughly ashamed.

Ted sat down on the bank to rest. The creek in front of him was too big to lose itself in the woods. It must flow somewhere and have a name. Its slow current seemed to be moving southward against the ruffling of the breeze, so he supposed it was one of the four or five tributaries of the Wading River. If his luck still held, and the name on the gravestone meant anything, this must be the water called "Hoquadunk Creek" in the old iron works deed.

" 'Beginning one mile south of Elder's Branch!' "

the boy repeated to himself. "All right—here goes."

He scrambled to his feet, crossed the boggy mouth of the smaller stream, and pushed on southward through an endless succession of swamps and thickets. There was abundant deer sign along the margin of the creek but no indication of hunting camps or trails. Ted had the strange, exciting feeling that he was moving through an undiscovered country.

However, his elation didn't last long. This was the toughest going he had ever encountered in the Pines. It took him a good ten minutes to struggle through a heavy tangle of cedar scrub, and no sooner had he fought clear than he plunged forward into swamp water up to his waist. Hastily he pulled the parcel of lunch out of his pocket, but the bread in the sandwiches was sopping wet. He held the sodden mass shoulder high and waded on, stumbling among the logs and muck that lay beneath the black surface. Behind him, Tramp barked twice, questioningly. The dog was still on dry ground and had no wish to swim again.

Ted hesitated. The water seemed to be growing deeper, and it stretched ahead, stagnant and forbidding under the gnarled cedar branches, as far as his eyes could reach. It was past noon. He was tired and hungry. Now that he had come so far he hated to turn back, but common sense told him it was useless to keep on. What he was following was only a wild hunch at best. He realized that it might take him hours to reach the other side of the swamp, and the farther he went, the harder it would be to retrace his steps.

Reluctantly he floundered back to the higher ground and looked around for a sunny place where he could sit down and dry his clothes. One bite of a wet sandwich took away his appetite, and he gave Tramp the rest of the bread and meat.

It was a disheartened youngster who pushed his way through the brush on the homeward trip. His hopes had soared when he found the little stream flowing into a larger creek, for it seemed certain he was on the trail of the Lost Forge. Now he was no longer confident. It might be mere chance that the old headstone bore the name of Jeremiah Elder—and he wasn't even sure that Elder was the name. Instead of having real news to give Lieutenant Gates, all he could report was guesswork. They were as far from finding the spies' hideout as ever.

At five o'clock he was stumbling wearily along the homeward trail beyond Woodmansie when a sound brought him up short in his tracks. Borne on the southerly breeze it reached him, faint but unmistakable, from a long way off—the thudding report of a shotgun. Holding his breath he listened. After five or six seconds it came again—*bang!* And a third shot followed almost immediately. Then silence shut down over the woods.

The boy stood there without moving for several minutes. A town-bred youngster might have thought a car had back-fired and paid no more attention. But Ted, raised in the Pines, wanted to know what lay back of things he heard and saw.

With the wind the way it was, he figured the shots might have come from as much as five miles to the southward. That would be well beyond the highway, in a section of the woods where nobody lived. Guns weren't fired without some cause. If it had been hunting season he could understand, but there was no game that could be shot in April. He was still trying to find an answer as he started off again toward home.

DOUBLE TROUBLE 2 m

6

EARLY THE NEXT MORNING TED SET
out for Muffin-Top Hill. His grandfather was still
worried about the smell of smoke in the air and
wanted news about the fire that was burning in the
woods to the south. As he had expected, the boy
saw Joe Lucas' bulky figure in the tower, and he was
soon on his way up the ladder. Pausing for breath at
the top, he pounded on the underside of the trap
door and the warden opened it for him.

"Hi, sonny," Lucas grinned. "What brings you

out this mornin'?"

"Grandpa is sort of anxious about that fire to the south," Ted explained. "He figures it's heading this way."

"Well," said the warden, "tell him there's no cause to fret yet. She's way down in Atlantic County an' ain't likely to cross the Mullica River. I jus' got word the boys were workin' all night an' claim to have it under control. We're safe up here unless another fire starts, though gosh knows it's dry enough for that!"

Ted looked through the glasses and saw only a dim gray haze over the Barrens, thirty miles and more to the southward. Reassured, he turned back to the warden.

"Say, Joe," he began, "did you hear guns shooting yesterday—late in the afternoon?"

"I hear a lot of 'em over Fort Dix way," Lucas answered. "Got so used to 'em I don't pay much attention."

"No—this was somewhere south. I reckon you'd have been too far away to hear, anyway. I was way down the other side o' Woodmansie an' there were three shots. Sounded like a duck gun."

Lucas yawned. "Somebody lettin' off at a hawk over his chicken-yard most likely," he offered, unimpressed. "Hello! Who's this in such a hurry?"

A dusty convertible, with the top up, came careening out of the woods along the ruts of the sand road. It slithered to a stop close to the foot of the tower and a red-haired man jumped out. "It's Bill Gates!" Ted exclaimed. "What do you suppose is up?" He pulled open the trap and stared down at the young army officer, now running up the steel ladder.

Gates barely nodded a greeting as he hoisted himself onto the platform. "Got to use your 'phone," he panted. "It's serious business, I'm afraid."

He picked up the receiver and gave the operator a number. After a moment's wait he spoke again with quiet urgency. "Major? J-21 reporting. Have they started to move that stuff yet? . . . Right! . . . Tomorrow is the day. I've got pretty clear evidence that yesterday was 'E' . . . No—just a case of canned goods. But a lot more had been taken away before I found the place. Any news from that truck? . . . Ten men ought to be enough—regulars if you've got 'em to spare . . . Yes, sir. I'll be there."

He put back the receiver and there was a look of relief on his sunburned face as he mopped his neck with a handkerchief.

"It's a bit of luck, finding both of you here at once," he smiled. "Things have been happening just a little too fast for me. It's all right, Ted. Joe's in on this, too. He's been working with me from the start."

Ted looked at the stout fire warden with new respect. "Gee," he said, reddening, "you must have wanted to smack me, Joe—the other day when I was talking big about—well, you know."

Lucas laughed. "I thought it was pretty smart o' you," he said, "even if you were dead wrong."

His sharp eyes went back to Gates. "You been in trouble, Lieutenant," he suggested. "Didn't I see some little round holes in the side o' your car when you druv in?"

It was Gates' turn to chuckle. "Yes," he said. "Buckshot. You don't miss much, do you? It's a long story but I'll make it short and be on my way. I was scouting around some of those old roads below the shore highway south of Cedar Creek. One place I saw fresh tire marks so I followed them in on an old sand track that I wouldn't have thought any car had used in twenty years. After a while I caught sight of a truck coming toward me. It was a C.C.C. truck, so I pulled out in the brush to let it go by. There were two men on the seat—white men, in ordinary working clothes. It wasn't till they were past that I remembered the only C.C.C. units down this way are colored boys.

"I got turned 'round in a hurry and started after them with my right foot on the floor. They were on a wider road by the time I caught up, and they were doing close to sixty. I pulled alongside and ordered them to stop. But right then a gun-barrel comes out from under the tarpaulin on the side, and a load of buckshot spatters over the car. The third blast got a front tire and I had to drop back or go into the ditch.

"It took about ten minutes to change the tire and get rolling again. Of course I'd lost them by then, but I got to a phone on the shore road and called headquarters so they could start the State Police looking for that truck. Thinking it over last night I wondered if maybe they'd been carrying in the supplies we'd heard about on the radio. So I went back to that old road the first thing this morning. It was fairly easy to follow the tire tracks. About a mile beyond where I'd met them, the truck had turned into the woods and plowed along through the brush for a way. I left the car and went on afoot —and by golly you were right, Ted! About the 'venison' and 'iron,' I mean. There was a swamp with red iron at the edge of the water and a deer path leading down to it. There were men's footprints in the muck, as if somebody had waded ashore. And sitting there under a bush, big as life, was a case of canned corn and tomatoes. The way I figure it, our friends with the hidden radio transmitter must have come in some kind of a boat to pick up the stuff. They had most of it loaded when they heard those shots and pushed off in a hurry, forgetting the last of their groceries."

Ted stood open-mouthed. For the moment he was speechless with excitement. "G-gosh!" he stammered at last. "Are you going after 'em?"

"Right away," the lieutenant nodded. "I'm taking a detail of men from the Fort. That's what I called up about. We've got to work fast because if yesterday was the 'E' day in that message, today's 'F' and 'G' must be tomorrow. And whatever their plan is, that's the day they've set to do the job."

"Could—" Ted choked—"could I come along with you?"

Gates looked at him. "No," he said sternly. "You just forget all I've told you, Ted, and keep on about your business. It won't be any place for a boy."

Ted was bitterly disappointed but he knew he was dealing with the Army and he had to obey orders. For an instant he was tempted to blurt out the story of his expedition the day before, but it seemed insignificant beside his friend's adventure.

"That swamp, now," said Joe Lucas. "Where you reckon that is, Lieutenant?"

"I never went there before," Gates answered, "and it's got no name, as far as I've heard. I'd say it lies right over there," he pointed. "Not more than seven or eight miles as the crow flies."

Lucas sighted along the pointing arm. "Section twenty-four," he nodded. "Let's take a look at the map."

All three of them bent their heads over the big geodetic survey chart. "Hm," said Lucas. "Plenty o' boggy land 'round there, looks like. They don't give a name to the creek that runs through, but it 'pears to be one o' the branches o' the Wadin'. I don't believe them Gov'ment fellers got their feet very wet when they did that part o' the surveyin'. They could see there were no hills more'n ten feet high an' they let it go at just markin' in a mess o' little swamps. Well, good luck to your hunt!"

"Thanks," said Gates. "We'll need it. I'd take along a walky-talky radio but it would be out of range of the Fort. If there should be any trouble we'll try to send up a little smoke. So take a look down that way with your glasses once in a while. If you get a signal from us, call the major. You know the number."

He shook hands with the warden, slapped Ted on the shoulder and grinned a farewell as he went down the ladder. From the platform the boy watched him walk, square-shouldered, across to his car, swing it around and vanish up the sand road in a cloud of dust.

"Gee!" he sighed. "What I'd give to be along with 'em! Reckon we won't know before tomorrow whether they catch those men, will we, Joe?"

"Can't tell," the warden frowned. "Sort o' wish they'd figured on takin' boats along, though. Those doughboys'll be wet up to the chin 'fore they get through wanderin' around in the swamp."

Ted thought of his own experience the day before. "That's right," he said soberly. "Still, Bill Gates knows what he's doing. I bet he'll bring 'em out if they're in there."

He left the tower a few minutes later and hiked home through the dry, hot woods. Knowing what was about to happen a few miles away made him restless. What a vacation this was turning out to be! And what a heap of things he would have to tell the gang at school when it was all over and he was released from his promise. He fairly danced along the trail in his excitement. Now that the shooting had started he was no longer afraid of what the spies might do. The Army was on the job and he had unbounded faith in Bill Gates.

Back at Creature Comfort Grandpa Winslow was fidgety. Even when Ted gave him reassuring news about the forest fire he scowled and stumped around the yard.

"Can't figure why it don't rain," he growled. "Goldurned well is so near dry the frogs have started to leave. We got to cooper up that big barrel that sits by the barn an' start hauling water or Doc an' Dotty are going to be mighty thirsty tomorrow. Not to mention you an' me an' Tramp an' the chickens."

Ted went over and looked at the barrel. It had lost two hoops and the staves were so loose he could see daylight between them. The old man went to the shed and began firing up his little forge. He was one of those independent Jacks-of-all-trades who could turn a hand to carpentry, blacksmithing or even cobbling shoes. Now he slipped a string around the barrel's top, used it to measure off a piece of strap iron from the pile of odds and ends in the corner, and pulled energetically on the homemade leather bellows that drove a blast of air through the forge fire.

In half an hour he had shaped the strap into a serviceable hoop, tested it on the barrel for size, and fastened the ends solidly with a white hot rivet. When the staves had been tapped into an even circle he slipped the hoop over the top like a collar and drove it down till it fitted solidly.

"There," he said. "Hitch up the horse an' take this contraption down to the creek. The water isn't clean enough to drink but it'll serve to wet up the wood. Sink her down good, so she'll swell. By tomorrow she ought to be tight enough to hold water an' you can go over to Mason's spring an' fill her up."

Between them they wrestled the old barrel onto the wagon bed and Ted drove down the woods trail to the creek. There he backed the tail of the wagon over the sloping bank to the water's edge, rolled the barrel off and pushed it down into the mud till it was nearly covered.

He spent the rest of that seemingly endless day trying to find jobs that needed doing around the place. Three or four times he almost gave way to his impulse and started off into the woods. It wasn't merely that he wanted to be present when the spies were caught. He had been piecing together the lieutenant's account with his own trip into the swamp and it struck him as possible that they had visited different parts of the same stream.

The place he had seen was north of the shore road, it was true, but it must be almost on a line with the location Gates had described, two or three miles to the south. And in that case maybe it *was* the Lost Forge that was being used as a hideout! Even if the tract mentioned in the deed began a mile south of Elder's Branch, nine thousand acres was a lot of land. It probably stretched on down the creek for miles, and the iron works could have been anywhere in that area.

But though his impatience to explore the swamp again was almost more than he could stand, he remembered Gates' warning and stayed at home through the long afternoon.

There was an ominous feel in the air that evening. A breeze still came fitfully from the south, but the heated atmosphere seemed heavy and threatening. The cow was fidgety when he brought her in for the milking, and he had to bury his forehead in her flank to keep her switching tail out of his eyes.

"So-o, boss," he murmured soothingly. "You act like a thunderstorm's coming. Hope you're right. We sure could use a little rain."

But when he mentioned the matter to his grandfather, the weatherwise old man shook his head.

"There's 'lectricity in the air," he admitted. "Won't rain, though. I can tell rain coming by the feeling in my leg—the one that isn't there. Rain always makes that foot kind o' prickly, but up to now I haven't noticed it."

Ted was still restless when bedtime came. There was no moon, but he knelt by his window staring out across the dark clearing toward the shadow of the woods. An owl hooted somewhere close by and Tramp barked hoarsely. Then the dog's voice subsided to a whimper and Ted could hear him panting and rattling his chain as he lay down again.

At first the boy thought there was something more behind these sounds than merely the restlessness of a hot night. He wondered if somebody might be approaching along the sand road through the woods. Perhaps Bill Gates had captured the men who were hiding in the swamp and was coming to let him know about it.

Then, when he had waited a while and no figure appeared in the clearing, another idea came to him. What if some of the spies had escaped? They might be prowling through the pines in the dark even now, bent on whatever mischief they had planned for tomorrow.

He had unlimited faith in the young lieutenant's ability, but this was no ordinary gang of criminals he was dealing with. They were clever and well organized and they were ready to kill if necessary.

After a long time the boy gave up his vigil and crept into bed. But even as he fell asleep he had the queer feeling that something was going to happen.

7

IT WAS NEARLY SUN-UP WHEN HE woke, and the rattle of pots and pans in the kitchen told him he had overslept. He dressed in haste and ran to the barn. Today was the big day. He was impatient to find out as soon as possible what success Bill Gates and his soldiers had had.

But when he brought in the milk Grandpa Winslow sensed his eagerness to be off. "Don't you forget there's a barrel o' water to haul, 'fore you go off any place," he reminded him.

Ted finished his breakfast and hurried out to harness the horse. His grandfather rode with him to the creek. "I knew 'twouldn't rain," he remarked, squinting at the hot and brassy sky. "We might get some in a day or two, though. 'Pears to me there's a change o' weather making."

They got the barrel out of the mud, rinsed it out and hoisted it aboard the wagon.

"Reckon she's tight enough now," said the old man. "Take along a couple o' buckets an' fill her right up to the top. That ought to last us two days if we're thrifty with it."

Mason's spring was a mile and a half to the westward in an abandoned clearing near the wood road. Old Doc had no intention of moving fast on a hot morning, and it took a good half hour to cover the distance at his plodding walk.

The spring itself wasn't much to look at. Choked with leaves and sticks, and almost hidden by brush, it lay at the foot of a small, wooded knoll. But when Ted had raked away some of the debris he could see clear water bubbling up from the white sand at the bottom.

He left the barrel on the wagon and began filling it, hurrying back and forth with a pail in each hand. It was a long and tiresome job. By the time he staggered out with the last two bucketfuls his arms were aching and he was glad to rest. He left the old horse to nibble at a tuft of grass and flopped down with his back against a tree.

Fifty yards away, an old wagon track ran across the clearing. It was overgrown with weeds and bushes and Ted had no idea where it led. He was speculating idly about this when a faint sound came from the woods south of the clearing. It was the throb of an automobile engine. The boy sat up quickly. It might be Bill Gates' car, and in that case he wanted to talk to him. He was starting to run toward the sound when he stopped in sudden amazement. Out of the woods came a good-sized truck, bumping northward along the abandoned track through the clearing. It had a tarpaulin stretched over bows for a top, and it was the same model as the government trucks he had seen working in Lebanon State Forest. But as it rattled past he saw that the side panel, where the big letters "C.C.C." should have appeared, was painted a shade of brown that didn't quite match the rest of the body. He caught only a moment's glimpse of the man at the wheel, but it showed him a squat, heavy-shouldered figure with a cap pulled far down over the eyes.

Ted had crouched in the bushes, motionless, as soon as the truck came in sight. The driver had not looked in his direction, and he didn't think he had been seen, though the horse and wagon were less likely to have escaped notice. In any case, the truck gave no sign of stopping. It chugged on, straight across the old clearing, and disappeared where the wagon track entered the woods to the northward.

The boy's brain was working fast now. He knew no truck or car had used that trail in many years. There could be only one reason why it was used now —to avoid more traveled roads. And the painted panel, where the Conservation Corps initials should have been—he knew he had to tell Gates about that in a hurry.

Ted jumped to the wagon seat and jerked so hard on the bit that the astonished old horse reared and bucked. Then the loose ends of the reins caught him across the rump and he set off at a clumsy gallop, the wagon bumping along behind him.

As soon as they reached the sand road leading toward home, Ted hopped off, looped the reins over the hames on Doc's collar and gave him another slap on the flank. "Giddap, there!" he said sharply. "An' keep going!"

He watched the horse trot off down the road with the precious barrel of water. Then he turned and started running in the opposite direction. The fire tower was only half a mile away and he wanted to get to that telephone fast.

Ted's breath was gone when he reached the open, sandy space at the foot of the tower. He expected to see the warden's old car parked in its usual place, but there was no sign of it. Panting, the boy began the long ascent. He was so winded after his run that he had to stop for a rest, two-thirds of the way to the top. As he clung there on the ladder he had a view northward over the treetops, and what he saw shocked him so that he nearly let go his hold.

A cloud of dark, heavy smoke was lifting above the woods, two or three miles away in the direction of Fort Dix. It increased every moment, rolling toward the reservation fence, pushed on by the dry south wind.

Shakily Ted scrambled the rest of the way to the top, pushed open the trap door and hauled himself up to the platform. He had to wait a few seconds to catch his breath and collect his wits. Then he lifted the telephone receiver and heard the operator's voice, calm and unhurried. "Number, please."

Swallowing hard, the boy gave her the number Gates had told him to memorize. In a moment another voice answered, crisp and masculine.

"I want to talk to J-21," Ted panted. "It's—it's awful important."

There was another delay of seconds that seemed like hours. Then, with deep relief, he heard Bill Gates speak. "This is J-21. Who's calling?"

"It's me—Ted. I'm at Muffin-Top—in the tower —an' there's a big fire starting, up toward the Fort. Bill—are you listening? I saw what looked like a C.C.C. truck heading up that way through the woods, about a quarter of an hour ago!"

Gates whistled. "That's it!" he said. "We missed 'em in the swamp. Listen, Ted—never mind the fire. There are plenty o' men to fight it—but we've got to catch those chaps that started it. I'll be right down there in my car. You watch for the truck. If it comes back, see where it's going. Keep it in sight if you—"

The voice stopped suddenly and there was complete silence on the wire. Ted jiggled the hook but nothing happened. Again and again he called into the transmitter without getting an answer. He didn't know much about telephones, but the fact that not even a hum came to his ear made him realize the line was dead. He hung up the receiver, stole another scared look at the menacing wall of smoke in the north, and went hurrying down the ladder.

Gates' orders were still ringing in his head. "Watch for the truck. See where it's going. Keep it in sight." He started running once more, and headed through the woods for the old Mason clearing.

Ted had gone hardly a hundred yards from the fire tower when he heard a pounding of heavy feet behind him. He turned, thinking it might be Joe Lucas. But the glimpse he caught through the brush showed him a stranger—a big, stocky man with close-cropped light hair. The boy ducked quickly behind a clump of bushes and waited while the man went lumbering past. He had on a gray shirt that clung to his body in dark, sweaty patches, and in his hand was something shiny—something that looked like wire-cutters. With a flash of understanding Ted remembered the dead telephone line. He knew he had just seen one of his country's enemies.

It was easy to follow the man's noisy progress through the woods. Crouching low and keeping far enough behind to avoid being seen, Ted ran after him, his naked feet making no sound among the sticks and brush.

The stranger was going in the exact direction Ted had planned to take, and—as it soon appeared—for the same reason. As they neared the clearing the boy heard the noise of an engine. The man in front of him stumbled out from the edge of the woods waving his arms, and the sound of the truck came closer. Ted saw it swerve out of the old grass ruts. It was rolling toward them across the bushy field.

There was no time to think, then. The truck was only a dozen yards away when the driver slammed on the brakes and shouted something in a guttural tongue that Ted couldn't understand. As the other man ran forward to climb into the cab, there was only one thought and one impulse in the boy's brain. He had to stay with that truck or risk letting the spies escape. Quick as a cat he darted toward the rear of the vehicle and pulled himself up on the open tail-gate just as it began to move.

He was so scared that his teeth were chattering. All he could do for a moment was hang on while the truck jolted over the uneven ground. Then the wheels slithered into sandy ruts again and the motion was easier. A tarpaulin that covered the back of the truck was tied down tightly at the corners. He lifted the loose edge in the middle and peered warily into the dark interior. It seemed to be empty except for some large metal cans that bounced and rattled when the going was rough.

Ted got his head under the stiff canvas and squirmed forward, little by little, till his shoulders were through. After that it was a simple matter to pull the rest of his wiry body inside. For a minute or two he lay without moving, waiting for his eyes to get used to the darkness. There was a strong smell of gasoline in the truck. He thought it came from the empty five-gallon cans, and he wondered if there wasn't a connection between those cans and the fire he had seen raging to the northward.

Through the narrow slit of daylight under the tarpaulin, Ted could catch occasional glimpses of sandy road and trees, but he couldn't be sure which direction the truck was taking. For the first few minutes he listened hopefully for the sound of Bill

Gates' car. Then he realized that his friend must have gone first to the fire tower. He tried to remember what he had told him before the telephone line was cut, but he didn't think he had mentioned Mason's clearing. That meant there would be no pursuit—no rescue. He was all alone on this job now!

The truck swayed and slewed in the sand, and tree-limbs whipped against its sides as they roared down the narrow, curving road. Ted resisted the temptation to crawl back to the tail-gate and drop off. He was so scared that his stomach felt like a small, tight knot in his middle, but the shame of knowing he wasn't brave kept him where he was. After all, the U. S. Army was depending on him, and he didn't want Bill Gates to find out he was afraid.

From time to time he could hear a rumble of voices coming from the cab. At least he might find out something about where he was going. He crawled forward a foot at a time along the lurching, jolting floor, and put his ear close to the metal panel. For a while the men were quiet. Then the one on the right—the big fellow Ted had followed through the woods—spoke.

"Think anybody saw you up there?"

The driver gave a gruff chuckle. "Na!" he said. "Dose shtupid fellas? It vas easy—no drick at all. I chust shpill der gas all ofer und shtrike a match. Foo—up she goes!"

"We ought to hear that ammunition dump go off pretty soon," the other replied. He spoke English like an American, but his words frightened Ted. Ammunition dump! Perhaps that was what Gates had meant when he asked the major if they had "started to move that stuff yet"! The boy shivered, expecting any instant to hear the earth-shaking report of an explosion that would rock the whole of South Jersey.

But as the slow minutes passed and nothing happened, his attention returned to the conversation in the cab. Most of it made little sense to him, but once in a while a sentence rang a bell in the boy's mind.

"You reckon Kurt an' Johnny got out all right?" It was the big man talking.

"Ya—sure! Ve find 'em down dere. Dose dumb Yankees giff up ven der vatter makes deep!"

The other man laughed. "Yeah," he said, "they sure looked like a pack o' drowned rats wadin' around in that swamp. An' they never even got close! We'll be able to use the place again if we want to."

Ted knew then that he was not to see the swamp hideout, after all. He had expected the truck would head in that direction, but he realized that they must have traveled considerably farther in the time that had passed since he climbed aboard.

"Easy, Jake," the man on the right warned the driver. "The highway's just past that bend. Better pull up here, out o' sight, an' let me go ahead. I'll let you know when the road's clear."

The truck stopped and Ted heard the big fellow climb down from the cab. Two or three minutes went by, and at last the vehicle began to rumble forward again. While it was still moving slowly the man who had been scouting the crossing scrambled back aboard. Then they picked up speed, rolled over a stretch of smooth concrete, and bumped along in sandy ruts once more. The boy lay on his stomach to look out under the tarp, but the glimpse of the highway he caught told him almost nothing. It was just a double strip of concrete running between pine woods, and there was no landmark to distinguish the crossing from a hundred others he had seen. From the slant of the sun, however, he was sure they were heading more to the east than to the south.

For three or four minutes the truck jolted on through thick woods. Then Ted heard a low, humming sound that he thought might be the distant drone of an airplane motor. The driver must have heard it, too, for there was a quick swerve to the left and a scraping of branches as the truck came to a sudden halt with the engine stopped.

"Ve got to hide, Gus," the guttural voice behind the wheel explained. "Dere's Army planes oudt. Der trees iss t'ick here, so ve stay a while, huh?"

"Yeah," the man called Gus replied uneasily. "Hope they didn't spot us first."

Ted lay very still while the men got out of the cab and stretched themselves. He heard the sharp scrape of matches being struck, and smelled cigarette smoke. Then came a casual remark from Gus that sent a chill of fear down the boy's spine.

"Hey, Jake," the fellow told his partner, "this oughta be a good place to get rid o' those gasoline cans."

8

FOR FOUR OR FIVE SECONDS THAT
seemed like an eternity, Ted lay in his dark corner
not daring to breathe. At any instant he expected
to see the tarpaulin lifted and if they found him
there he knew his chances weren't worth a plugged
nickel.

"Vait," Jake answered. "Plenty time ven der
planes iss gone. Dose cans makes too shiny in der
sun."

The boy inside the truck let a long, shivering

breath escape him. The discovery of his hiding-place was postponed for a while at least. Still he dared not move. The men seemed to be strolling aimlessly around, but they were never more than a few feet from the truck. Occasionally he heard one of them yawn or make some low-voiced remark. And every so often the ominous droning of a plane would grow louder, then fade again in the distance.

Ted's mind shook free of the paralysis that had seized it. He considered a number of wild plans for attracting the attention of those Army fliers. The driver, Jake, had mentioned the shiny cans. Couldn't he get out with one of them—reach an open place among the trees and flash some kind of message? But the futility of this scheme became apparent a moment later when one of the men leaned creakingly on the tail-gate and lighted another ciga-rette.

The sound of the scratching match gave Ted a different idea. If he had any matches of his own he might contrive to empty a few drops of gasoline against the tarp and set the truck afire. In the excitement that was sure to follow he thought he would have a chance to escape, and the smoke would be seen by the searching planes. With noiseless haste he felt in all his pockets, but there was not a single match to be found. When he had time to think it through a little farther he realized that the plan was foolhardy anyway. He would merely be starting another forest fire, and the two men would have time to get away before any pursuers could reach the spot.

Hours dragged by and still the truck stayed hidden under the pine branches. From the scraps of talk he could overhear, Ted guessed that the pair outside were in no hurry to start again. They seemed to be well satisfied with their morning's work and willing to wait for dusk to cover their retreat.

The scouting planes still went over at irregular intervals. The boy felt grateful to Bill Gates for keeping them at it, but it was increasingly hard to lie there on the hard truck-bottom without moving. His legs went to sleep and he shifted his position with painful slowness. As the afternoon neared its end he was thirsty, too, and hungry. But what bothered him most was the fear that one of the men loafing beyond the tarpaulin would remember those gasoline cans. Now that the sun was low there was no reason why they should put off disposing of them.

At length he heard heavy footsteps close to the side of the truck. "Come on, Jake, let's get movin'," came the surly voice of the big, crop-haired man. "There ain't been a plane over in half an hour. Besides, it's gettin' dark anyhow. I didn't eat since five o'clock, an' I got to have some grub."

To Ted's intense relief the driver made no objection. He heard them clambering into the cab, the starter grunted and the engine took hold with a roar. A moment later they had backed out into the sand road and were chugging forward again.

Now was his chance to get away if he wanted to, but he discovered he didn't want to. Having lived through that grim afternoon, he had a strange detached feeling about his own safety. These men in the truck with him were enemies of everything he believed in—dangerous to America as a pair of rat-tlesnakes. If he quit now and saved his own hide, they would almost certainly go scot-free. They'd join the rest of their gang and be ready to carry out fresh acts of sabotage.

No—he was going to see this thing through. The dusk seemed to be shutting down earlier than usual and Ted thought it might be clouding up for a rain. Then he crawled to the rear of the truck and looked out under the edge of the tarp. There were dark clouds hiding the sunset light in the west, but they weren't rain clouds. Along their lower edge a red glow flickered. The forest fire south of the Fort Dix reservation was raging now on a front that must be eight or ten miles long. He wondered with a pang of terror what his grandfather would do if the flames swept toward Creature Comfort. The old man would be worried about him, too. He was pretty sure old Doc had trotted home with the water bar-rel, but there had been no chance to send a note or any other sort of message. Maybe Bill Gates had stopped by the clearing and told about hearing from

Ted, but that was a slim chance. The boy could imagine how busy Gates had been all day.

There was still light enough to see the road and the country on either side. Ted realized that there were no longer any tall woods in sight. The low brush and stunted oaks and pines had a familiar look. The Plains! He figured they must have traveled twenty miles in all, and their direction had been east or southeast. That would mean they were somewhere in the wilderness west of Forked River and north of Cedar Bridge. The road was very old and rough—a forgotten track that the spies must have hunted out for just such a purpose as this escape.

Lying on his stomach, staring out under the edge of the canvas, Ted saw low, desolate, brush-covered hills rolling away to the north. He had heard of the Forked River "Mountains" but he had never been so close to them before. More than a century had passed since these hills had given hiding to gangs of deserters and cutthroats, but an evil reputation still clung to the place.

The truck crept along at a cautious pace, mile after mile. Ted could not be certain, from his place at the rear, but he thought they were driving without lights.

At the end of an hour they came to another halt and he heard Gus get out of the cab and walk off in the darkness. There was a new smell in the night breeze that blew fitfully from the southeast— a smell of salt marshes. Ted sniffed it again and again and knew he wasn't mistaken. They were nearing the sea. He had a sudden feeling of loneliness for he knew now that he was a long way from home.

After a time the big man must have given some kind of signal, for Jake let in the clutch and the truck began moving ahead. After Gus was back in the cab they crossed another concrete highway that must be the shore road from New York. Ted caught a momentary gleam of far-off car lights, but before they came close the truck was already hidden in the woods on the other side.

The last five miles of that ride were the roughest

of the whole journey. Low-growing trees and bushes scraped the sides of the truck, and the road, if it could be called a road, was cut by gulleys and drifted with loose sand. Occasionally the wheels slithered through tidal mud in low spots where the salty, fishy smell rose stronger than ever.

Finally the vehicle eased over a couple of bumps and stood still. The engine stopped. Holding his breath to listen, Ted heard the two men dismount from the cab and go tramping off through the sand. He caught the sound of low voices, and then a door creaked open and shut again.

He thrust his head out from under the tarp, looked in both directions, and crawled out over the tail-gate with as little noise as possible. His eyes were used to the darkness. Thirty or forty feet away he saw a low, dilapidated-looking building, half hidden by thickets and low, gnarled cedars. Beyond it there was water—a broad expanse of it with gray-black waves lapping gently along the reedy shore. Dim in the distance he could make out another black line of land, with the sea beyond it. He was somewhere along the edge of Barnegat Bay. The house, he thought, must be a fisherman's shack.

At first it seemed that the building was completely dark. Then Ted moved a step or two and caught a glimpse of a thin line of light under the door. The windows were blackened by some kind of thick curtains.

Tiptoeing through the sand, he reached a corner of the house and crouched against it under the shelter of a sweet-scented bayberry bush. Faintly he could hear the creak of floor boards as men moved about inside. There was a rumble of voices, too, and occasional laughter. Then, only a foot from Ted's ear, through the weathered shingles and flimsy planking came a different voice, clear and resonant. Someone had turned on a radio.

". . . Eastern Standard Time. We now bring you a résumé of the latest news. The forest fire raging south of Fort Dix was still only partially under control at eight o'clock tonight. Six thousand men of the Forty-fourth Division and other detachments of troops have been fighting the flames almost without rest since it was discovered at nine-thirty this morning. All munitions have been moved to safety and only two unimportant buildings inside the reservation have been burned, it is officially reported. Sweeping northward in an area over five miles long, the fire has destroyed several thousand acres of woods and a number of dwellings. So far no deaths are known to have occurred. Owing to the extremely dry season the forest burned like tinder and wherever sparks were blown fresh flames sprang up almost instantly. Fire wardens and officers reported that it was impossible to control backfires, and therefore the troops have had to concentrate on broadening the fire lines with axes and shovels. There is strong suspicion of sabotage in the fact that the fire apparently started a long distance from any traveled road or house. Army officers so far refuse to make any statement on this point but there has been great activity on the part of intelligence units throughout the day. It is reported on good authority that arrests of a number of suspects may be made before midnight. Meanwhile all roads leading away from the area of the fire have been watched by a strong cordon of State Police, and it is doubtful that any fifth columnist who may have started the fire has been able to escape.

"Now for the news from Washington. This afternoon Congress . . ."

The radio clicked off and Ted heard a gruff chuckle inside the shack. "You see any State Police on the way out, Jake? Haw, haw! Say, we forgot those cans in the truck. Get a shovel an' we'll bury 'em back in the sand."

Ted crawled farther back into the bushes and lay flat on his stomach. He saw a brief glow of light as the door was opened. Then two shadowy figures moved across the sandy space to the truck. They unfastened the tarp and lifted out the gasoline cans. There was a sound of digging, a few yards back in the brush, and after a short time the pair returned to the house.

The boy wondered what he should do next. It seemed that he had found the headquarters of the spy gang. If he could be sure they planned to stay there he ought to get to a telephone and send word to Bill Gates. But it must be four or five miles back to the highway and even there he could not be sure of finding a house. Meanwhile the enemy agents in the shack might be planning to clear out. If he could hear more of their talk perhaps he could make sure.

Working back along the wall of the building, he pressed his ear against the shingles and listened. There was a conversation going on, but he could make out none of the words. Two men were speaking in a foreign language. Then he heard the big fellow called Gus interrupt. He sounded impatient.

"What's he sayin', Jake? I never could understand the lingo very good."

"Der boat," Jake answered. "Ve send a message in two hours. She come sure in der mornin'."

"Oh, that so? Well, I'm goin' to have another cup o' coffee."

The words made Ted hungrier and thirstier than ever. But he was even more interested in what Jake had said about the boat. They must have a radio transmitter in the shack. And somewhere outside a boat was waiting to take them off as soon as it got their signal. It would be there in the morning, according to Jake. That meant the gang would stay hidden the rest of the night, and it gave Ted five or six hours to summon help. He didn't wait to hear any more but went quietly past the truck and felt his way toward the road.

Until he was stumbling along that rough track in the dark, he had not realized how tired he was. Sand-burs pricked his toes and twigs thrust at his face. In the low places, wet sticky mud gripped at his ankles. There had been a few mosquitoes singing about his head and arms when he was lying beside the house. Now they seemed to rise in clouds from the marsh. He thought of himself as a tough-skinned Piney, indifferent to insect bites, but there was a bitter ferocity in the attack of these salt-water monsters. Before he could slap them off, they raised puffy welts on his forehead, cheeks and neck.

It was so dark now that he had to feel before him, parting the brush with his hands in places where it grew out over the road. After a while it seemed to him that the track was even narrower than he remembered. Measuring with his arms he found it hard to believe that the truck could have gone through. He wondered if there might be a fork in the road and if he had taken the wrong branch. There was no way to be sure, so he plodded on.

Uncertainty plagued him now. Several times he stopped, fighting mosquitoes and trying to recall the location of those humps and gulleys. He had no idea how much time had passed since he left the spies' hangout but it must be hours.

Finally he found himself definitely off the road. There was no opening in the bushes ahead of him or to either side. He turned, discouraged, to retrace his steps, and moved perhaps a dozen yards on what he thought was the way back. Then a clump of black, spreading juniper clawed at his eyes and he found his path blocked once more.

Ted had been lost more than once in his life, but always in daylight and in a kind of woods that were familiar to him. Now a feeling of helplessness bowed his shoulders, adding to the misery of hunger, thirst and mosquito bites.

After a minute he mastered the panic that had seized him. He had a job to do and he wasn't going to let this mishap get him down. He stood back and took a look above him, hoping to get a bearing from the stars. But the sky was dark with a scud of clouds drifting in from the sea. Even that might help him, he thought, if he knew the direction of the wind. If it was still from the south he needed only to keep it on the left side of his face and sooner or later he would reach the highway to the westward.

With this plan to buoy his spirits he turned and began fighting his way through the brush. Sometimes the breeze was so light that he couldn't feel it. Then he would stand still, try to wet a finger in his parched mouth, and hold it up patiently till he caught the next stir of air.

Breaking through thickets of cedar and bayberry and wading across reed-covered tidal swamps was exhausting work and slow. He kept going for what seemed like miles and still the brush and the marsh and the swarming mosquitoes surrounded him. He began to grow desperate. The night was passing and he knew it might take hours for Gates and his men to reach the hiding place, even after he had found a telephone.

Ted didn't know much about malaria but he knew now that he must have a fever. His skin felt hot and dry and at times he was lightheaded. He would find his mind straying queerly and that frightened him. By a stern effort of will he got control of his faculties again and plunged ahead with the energy of desperation. Over and over he told himself that if he could keep going long enough he was bound to come out somewhere.

Once he tried to drink some of the water from a little stream he crossed, but its brackish taste was so strong that he spit it out again. Then for a long time he wandered on, half conscious, knowing only that he dared not stop. Finally the breeze died altogether and thick fog settled like a blanket over the marsh.

Unable to see more than a few feet, and completely bewildered as to directions, Ted gave up then. He crawled out of the muck to a hillock of dry sand under a cedar clump and lay there, too tired to care what happened. In a moment the sleep of exhaustion drugged him into unconsciousness.

9

IT WAS THE DAWN WIND, BLOWING
cold off the sea, that roused Ted, hours later. He
sat up, blinking and shivering, unable at first to remember where he was or how he got there. The fog
was gray with early daylight now, and beginning
to lift in curling, wraith-like streamers.

The boy saw that his shirt was torn almost to
ribbons and stained red from the scratches on his
body. The mosquitoes must have had a feast while
he slept, for his face felt queer and lumpy when he

passed a hand over it. The nightmare of his journey across brush and marsh came back to him vividly then and he got stiffly to his feet, staring around him.

He saw that by some turn in his wanderings he had come once more to the edge of the bay. Right in front of him the tide had risen to cover the flats and waves were slapping against the shore a dozen yards away. Even while he watched, the rising mist disclosed a mile-wide stretch of water and the dunes of the island beyond. At the rim of the milk-white sea the sun was coming up in a pale disk of light.

Then Ted's heart gave a sudden leap, for he saw two things, almost at the same instant. One was a weatherbeaten, flat-bottomed boat, pulled up in the reeds on his left. The other was a fluttering speck of red-white-and-blue bunting, slowly climbing to the top of a mast, across on the island!

Shading his eyes with his hand, he could make out the cupola and buildings of a Coast Guard station just below the flag. There would be a telephone there, and men who knew how to deal with enemies. Forgetting all about his thirst and hunger, Ted scrambled toward the rowboat. It probably belonged to some bay fisherman or crabber, but this was no time to worry about using another person's property.

The boy jerked the rope from the stake to which it was tied, heaved with all his strength on the bow of the heavy old craft, and moved it toward the water a foot at a time. When he had it almost afloat he remembered that he would need oars. There were none in the boat and a hasty search of the near-by reeds and bushes failed to reveal any. But Ted was too close to victory to let that stop him. He wrenched the forward thwart loose and held it up in both hands. It was an awkward thing to paddle with, but a lot better than his bare hands. A final push sent the boat into the water. And in a moment the boy was sitting astern, wielding his heavy board with might and main.

After he got the hang of it, he was able to guide the clumsy craft through the waves on a fairly straight course. His progress was slow, but he could tell by sighting past the cedars on shore that he was making headway.

He had started from a brush-covered point, jutting out into the bay. Though there were no houses in sight he saw a little wisp of smoke rising above the woods, a mile or two away to the north, and he wondered if it might come from the spies' shack.

It seemed an endless time before he could tell himself he was halfway across. Then the shore of the island drew rapidly closer as the wind lightened and the tide carried him in. He saw a low wooden pier with two or three boats tied to it and steered in that direction.

There was nobody in sight when Ted made fast the painter and clambered up on the rickety dock. He ran along it to a sandy path that led over the dunes. At the top he could see the Coast Guard station right in front of him, a hundred yards away on the other side of the empty highway. In his haste he stumbled in the loose sand and pitched on his face in the wiry dune grass, but he hardly noticed the mishap. Every ounce of his energy was concentrated now on getting his news to the neat white buildings ahead.

The door opened as he panted up to the steps. A big man with a gray beard and shining brass buttons on his blue uniform was staring down at him in some surprise.

"Well, sonny," the man's deep voice boomed, "what's up? Spotted a wreck, have ye?"

Now that Ted had reached the place, he had trouble finding words to say. A wave of shyness tied his tongue as he realized that no stranger could be expected to believe his story. But there was a twinkle in the big man's steel blue eyes, and at last the boy knew he had to say something.

"Cap'n—" he gulped, dry-mouthed and hollow-voiced—"I got to get to a telephone. It's—it's government business an' awful important. Only first I guess I need a drink o' water, 'cause I haven't had any since yesterday morning."

The Coast Guard officer not only looked as if he believed him but he took immediate action. "Right here, son," he said, and led the way back through a big room into a lavatory. In a moment he was holding out a full glass of water which Ted accepted with trembling hands.

He sipped it slowly, letting its delicious coolness trickle into his parched throat. But he didn't ask for a second glass. "Do you mind if I telephone?" he said. "It's for the Army Intelligence."

The big man's bushy eyebrows went up, but he accepted Ted's statement. "Right here at the desk," he said, pointing to the instrument.

Ted picked it up gingerly. It was a hand set, different from anything he had ever used.

"You talk in this end," the officer told him gravely.

"Number, please," came the operator's voice, and Ted gave her Bill Gates' number.

The next voice he heard was a man's. "Yes," it said guardedly. "Who did you want?"

"J-21," said the boy.

"Sorry, he's not here. But he said there might be a call. Who's this speaking?"

"Ted Winslow."

"Good! Just a minute. I'll give you the major."

Ten seconds passed and a brusque, clipped voice came on the wire. "Yes? What have you to report, Winslow?"

"The men that started the fire," Ted answered. "I was supposed to watch where they went. So when the truck came past, I—I got on the back. There were a lot o' gasoline cans in it—empty, an' the driver talked funny, like a foreigner. They talked about how they poured gas around an' set fire to the woods. When the planes began to come over they hid the truck under some pines, an' didn't come out till it got dark. Then they drove over an old road through the Forked River Mountains an' got to a place where the rest o' the gang were—in a shack right on the edge o' the bay. Yes, sir— Barnegat Bay, I reckon."

He glanced up at the big Coast Guard officer and got a nod of assent.

"Are they still there?" the major asked.

"Yes, sir. I listened through the wall o' the house an' heard 'em say they were going to send for a boat to take 'em off this morning. Then I set out to try to find the highway, but I got lost. When it came daylight I got across the bay to the Coast Guard station, an' here I am."

The man beside him reached out a big hand for the telephone. When Ted gave it to him he smiled and began speaking into the transmitter.

"This is Chief Bosun's Mate Kelso of the Cedar Beach station, Major," he boomed. "Yes, I'd say the boy's tellin' the truth. He sure looks like he'd been out in the marsh all night. Anyhow, I believe him enough so I'm goin' to call Cape May an' get a cutter up here to head off that boat. You will? Good!"

He turned to Ted. "'Bout where along shore d'you reckon this shack is?"

"I think it must be the other side o' that point, to the north," he said. "There was chimney smoke over there this morning."

"Major?" Mr. Kelso resumed. "You'll find the road somewhere between Barnegat an' Manahawkin—likely nearer Barnegat. We'll try an' hold 'em from this side. Right! Good-by, Major."

He hung up then, but his hand was still on the telephone as he glanced at Ted again. "Seems to me you look a bit peaked, son," he said kindly. "You march out in the galley an' tell the cook I sent you for some breakfast. While you're stokin' your boiler I'll call the Cape May base. Your Army friends are on the job, an' they're goin' to cover the land side."

Ted needed no second invitation to breakfast. He found that the "galley" was a big, spotless kitchen where a burly, white-aproned man with tattooed arms was breaking eggs into a sizzling frying pan. He must have heard the captain's order, for he grinned at Ted and motioned to a chair at a small table under the window.

"Hiya, kid," he said. "There'll be some chow on the plate in a couple o' shakes. Milk's in that pitcher. Go to it."

The boy felt better when he had finished a glass of milk, and he was ready to do full justice to the bacon and eggs and cornbread that followed.

Half an hour later three men came in from their early patrol of the beach and others went out to take their places. Mr. Kelso asked Ted a few more questions, then ordered the bosun's mate, his second in command, to mount a machine gun in the launch and have the engine warmed up.

"The *Cayuga* started up from Cape May soon as I called," he explained to the boy. "But it'll be ten o'clock before she can reach the inlet. We may see a little action while we're waitin' for her. Why don't you go aloft with the lookout? You can see all that goes on from up there."

Ted was grateful for the suggestion, for the waiting had begun to make him fidgety. At the head of the ladder-like stairs he found himself in a bright, square room, the sides of which were all windows. A young seaman was scanning the open sea with a pair of binoculars. His first remark showed that he was fully acquainted with Ted's story.

"No way of telling just what kind of a craft she'll be," he said. "But I've got my eye on a sail out yonder. Two-masted schooner off there to the east-

'ard. See her?"

Ted didn't need the glasses. Almost in the path of the sun and four or five miles out from shore he could see her gray sails. She was still hull down but coming fast with a favoring wind.

"Way she moves, I reckon she's got an auxiliary engine," the lookout continued. "Ought to be near the inlet in another half hour, an' she's headed right for it."

Ted watched the schooner's approach for a few minutes, then went to the other side of the cupola. There was a gray haze in the northeast, beyond the low, wooded horizon line.

"Is the fire still bad up there?" he asked. "It's so far off I can't tell."

"No, they've got it pretty well under control," the seaman answered. "Heard on the radio this morning they figure Fort Dix is safe anyhow. Say— looks like Cape May's on the job! Here comes a patrol plane."

High over the sea to the southward, Ted saw a silvery speck. It drew swiftly nearer, the roar of its twin motors coming clearly through the open windows. Flying at a height of three or four thousand feet, the seaplane passed directly over the schooner and proceeded on up the coast.

The sailing craft was near enough now so that they could see her hull through the glasses.

"I'd take her for an ordinary fisherman," the lookout remarked. "Got a couple o' dories nested on deck an' what looks like a mess o' nets aft. There's still a few come in here under sail—mackerel boats from New England, mostly. If she's makin' for the inlet it's lucky for her the tide's high. Two or three hours more an' there won't be much water over the bar."

"Gosh," said Ted, "how long do you s'pose it'll take the cutter to get here? Can a big ship like that get over the bar?"

"No. She wouldn't try it even at the top o' the tide. But you can bet she's makin' all the knots she's got. Ought to be about three hours from the time she started till she passes us. She'll be close enough to stop the other feller from comin' out, though."

The schooner drove straight for the inlet, five

miles northward, where Ted could see the lonely shaft of Barnegat Light standing guard at the head of the island. It was a minute or two after nine o'clock when her foresail passed behind the light-house tower. Then they saw her veer southwest through Clam Island channel and come down the bay with the wind on her beam.

While Ted was watching this maneuver he heard the hum of an engine and turned to look southward. Up the road from the Manahawkin bridge a car was coming at racing speed. He gave a yell of joy and started down the ladder, for he had recognized the dusty black convertible.

By the time he reached the door, Bill Gates was getting out of his car. The lieutenant's clothes were rumpled and soot-stained and his face showed lines of fatigue, but he grinned when he caught sight of Ted.

"Well!" he said, shaking hands. "For a while, there, yesterday, I was sort of worried about you, old-timer!"

"Is Gramps all right? Did you get a chance to

see him?" Ted asked.

"Sure—he's spry as a three-year-old. The fire didn't come within half a mile of the clearing, and he said he knew you'd gone off on some sort of a wild goose chase when the horse came home alone. But tell me some more about that truck-ride of yours. Did you get a look at the men? And how did you manage to keep from being seen?"

Ted spent the next few minutes answering the questions Gates shot at him, and did his best to describe the location of the fishing shack on the bay shore.

The young Intelligence officer seemed satisfied. "There are three or four little roads into those woods and we brought enough men to keep 'em all covered," he said. "What about the boat? Seen anything of it yet?"

"There's a schooner crossing the bay right now," Ted told him, "and we think that's the one. Come on up in the tower."

They met Kelso at the foot of the stairs and Ted introduced him to his friend. Even as the two men were shaking hands, a hail came down to them from the lookout.

"*Cayuga's* in sight, sir! And the schooner's putting in for the point above Gunning River!"

10

TED DARTED UP THE LADDER, CLOSELY
followed by Gates and the Coast Guard officer. The
cutter was still hardly more than a smudge of smoke
on the southern horizon, but across the bay the
headsails of the schooner were clearly visible above
the sedgy point.

"That's the place!" Ted nodded. "I must've
hiked all over that point last night. I can see how
I got turned 'round, though. I figured the wind was
still south, but it was more easterly."

The bosun's mate came up to report that the launch was ready, and Kelso gave orders for four men to take their rifles and run her over to the point, prepared for possible trouble. Bill Gates took command of the party.

Ted would have given almost anything to go with them, but the lieutenant sternly forbade it. "Right here's the safest place for you, young game-cock," he said. "You'll have a near enough view of it, if there's any action."

Four or five minutes later Ted saw the launch pull out from her boathouse on the bay shore, and head northward at a good clip. The machine gun mounted in her bows gave the little craft a business-like look.

While she was still in sight off the point, the patrol plane came droning back down the coast. They saw the silver ship circle twice above the *Cayuga,* then proceed southward toward Cape May.

There was a quarter of an hour of restless waiting after that. The launch ran close to the point, skirted it and disappeared behind one of the small, reedy islands. The cutter, steaming at her best speed of close to twenty knots, still seemed to Ted's impatient eyes to be crawling. She was nearly abreast of the station now, and not much more than a mile offshore. Through the glasses the boy could easily see her gun crew working like ants around the forward four-inch gun.

"The cap'n's been talkin' to her," the lookout told Ted. "We've got a little wireless set below, an' one o' the seamen knows how to send. Guess the skipper's told 'em the schooner's inside an' they've taken battle stations."

The words gave Ted a prickly feeling down his spine. They had a fairly grim sound. He began to wonder how Bill Gates and the sailors would fare if it came to a real sea-fight. Still the slow minutes ticked by. The boy divided his attention between the mainland shore and the *Cayuga*, now making in toward Barnegat Inlet.

He had just turned eastward to look at the cutter when a dull, thudding sound came to his ears. For a second he didn't know what direction it came from. Then the lookout touched his arm.

"Over there," he said, pointing across the bay. "They've fired on the launch."

The man's voice was calm and steady as he gave his news to the officer, but there were hard lines around his mouth. Ted stared at the rising cloud of white smoke beyond the point and waited for a second report, but none sounded. Kelso came quickly up the ladder.

"Did you hear any noise o' machine gun fire?" he asked.

"No, sir."

The officer stroked his beard. "Wouldn't hear it anyhow, with the wind as 'tis," he growled. "Wish I'd gone along. Looks like sure enough trouble. Well, I'll pass the word to Cap'n Bronson on the *Cayuga*."

Ted felt as if he could hardly bear it, up there in the cupola, and yet there was nothing he could do to help. For a moment he considered running up the island to a place where he could see the cove beyond the point. But he realized he would have to go nearly two miles to reach such a spot and meanwhile he might miss some of the action.

Almost as soon as he had made his decision he found reason to be glad he had stayed. The lookout, with his glasses trained on the point, reported that the schooner's masts were coming into sight above the low-growing cedars. At his hail the officer came aloft again. In silence they watched the swiftly moving topsails of the stranger craft as she swung out into the open bay. There was a good breeze on her quarter, but the foaming wake she left proved that the auxiliary engine was adding knots to her speed.

Kelso had binoculars of his own, and as he turned them in the direction of the cutter he gave a quick exclamation.

"Bronson's put two boats over!" he said. "They're pullin' for the inlet now. Looks like we've got those fellers in a pretty tight corner!"

Borrowing the lookout's glasses, Ted could see the heave and flash of the oars as the white boats rose to the Atlantic swell. They were so close to the inlet now that after a moment both were hidden by the dunes. The cutter was standing by in the deeper water off the bar.

"Somethin's bound to happen pretty quick—headin' straight for each other that way," Kelso rumbled. "Right now the schooner hasn't sighted 'em, but she will, soon as she clears that island."

They waited tensely for a minute, two minutes, and saw the sailing vessel come suddenly into the wind, her jibs fluttering. She hung there for a few seconds before her sails snapped taut once more and the bow-wave began to curl white under her forefoot. She was headed back for the cove!

"Must've spotted the cutter's boats," the officer commented. "Don't believe she could see the *Cayuga* from where she came about, but she knew what two boats full o' bluejackets meant."

"Take a look at her, sir," the seaman put in. "Where she had those nets piled up aft—they're gone now an' she's got a gun mounted—"

"Right!" said Kelso. "Pretty fair-sized gun. Close to a three-incher, looks like. She could have sunk the launch with that one shot!"

Ted shivered. He had a vivid mental picture of Bill Gates, maybe badly hurt, trying to swim ashore in that cold water.

"Couldn't we get over there somehow an'—an' see?" he asked, timidly.

"Huh?" grunted the officer. "Yes, just what I was thinkin'. I'll try an' round up enough men to make a boat crew."

Five minutes later they were jogging along the path over the dunes—Kelso, Ted and two husky young seamen. Ted could still hardly believe the officer meant to let him come, but so far he hadn't been told to stay behind.

There was a skiff with two pairs of oars racked up in the boathouse. They swung it into the water and the seamen jumped to the rowing thwarts. Kelso took his place in the stern and watched Ted scramble down beside him without comment. With a lusty heave on the oars, the crew shot their light craft out into the channel.

Boom! Over the dunes rolled the report of a heavy gun, and Ted saw a column of spray rise close to the schooner, scudding along two miles to the north.

Kelso chuckled. "Must be they're in sight from the cutter's crow's-nest," he said. "She's firin' across a low place in the island. That ought to scare 'em plenty."

Another shot fell a few yards astern of the schooner and she plunged ahead like a rabbit going for its burrow. There was no more firing after that. Three or four minutes later the enemy craft clawed her way in behind the point and they could only see her swiftly moving topsails. The two boats from the cutter were pulling steadily across the bay in pursuit, but they fell farther behind with every sweep of the oars.

"Keep goin', boys. Put some back in it," Kelso growled to his rowers. "We want to get there as soon as the *Cayuga's* party."

They cut in close to the point, the port oars swishing through dry stalks of sedge. The low, marshy shore seemed to stretch endlessly ahead. Ted could understand now how he had wandered half the night in that expanse of brush-grown wilderness.

The oarsmen panted and the sweat ran down their tanned faces, but they kept up the fast stroke. They were close to the entrance of the cove when the cutter's boats swung by, almost within hailing distance. As the skiff rounded the upper end of the point Ted leaned forward, eager to see what might be going on at the spies' landing place.

The first thing he saw was the schooner. She was lying in shoal water close to the shore, her masts canted far over to leeward.

"Beached her, by golly!" Kelso rumbled. "They're tryin' to get away overland!"

Two or three distant figures could be seen scurrying back and forth from the schooner to the shore. They were wading through water that reached to their armpits and carrying bundles of assorted shapes balanced on their heads.

"What have they got to travel in?" Kelso asked. "Cars, maybe?"

"All I saw in the dark was that truck," Ted replied. "But they might ha' had a car hid in the bushes. Gosh—the launch isn't anywhere in sight. You reckon they really did—"

The sharp crack of a forty-five caliber pistol interrupted him. It was answered almost instantly by scattered fire from the fishing shack, now visible among the bushes.

"That's some of our boys," said the captain grimly. "Whatever happened to the launch, they didn't all get put out of action."

Ted caught a glimpse of a brown-clad figure crouching behind a thick clump of bushes and saw the flash as the automatic barked again. That was Bill Gates. He was a good hundred yards from the shack—too far to hope for anything but a lucky hit. Still he banged away, trying apparently to keep the spies busy until the cutter's boats could get up. There were rifles in those boats, Ted could see, and they were nearly close enough now for accurate shooting.

The men had abandoned the schooner and there was nobody in sight between the shack and the

shore. Then came the roar of the truck engine starting. Gates stood up, pointed toward the camp and
shouted something to the officer in the nearest
boat. As the truck lumbered into momentary view
beside the building, rifles cracked from the boat's
bow.

"The engine's out o' business!" yelled Ted.
"Look—they're getting out!"

The truck had lurched to a stop and four or five
men were running from it, taking cover behind the
house again. The seamen in the boats gave a cheer,
but at that moment a small gray sedan chugged out
across the open space and disappeared in the woods
before another shot could be fired.

By this time the skiff was close enough for Ted
to hear Gates' words as he waved the boats on.
"Some of 'em are still there," he called. "And
they're armed, so don't take the boats in too close.
Better land this side and surround 'em."

The young ensign in the stern-sheets of the nearest boat acknowledged the advice with a stiff salute
and steered for the shore. The other craft veered

off to make a landing on the farther side of the shack.

"Ahoy there, Gates!" the Coast Guard officer bellowed. "Where are the rest o' the men?"

A bedraggled-looking life-saver sprang out from the thicket and answered the hail. "All here, sir," he called. "We lost the launch when they put a shot through her bows, but we got ashore an' nobody's hurt."

Bill Gates grinned and waved his arm. His wet khaki shirt clung in wrinkles to his body. "Hi, Chief!" he shouted. "I see that young passenger of yours is still looking for trouble. Sorry about your launch and gun, but I think they can be salvaged. See you when this is over."

With that he started toward the shack, slipping a fresh clip of cartridges into his automatic as he ran.

Kelso gave a grunt. "Set me ashore," he ordered the rowers. "You stay here with the boy till I signal you."

The big man was unarmed but he appeared to have no fear of bullets. A moment later he had taken command of the launch crew, looked over the two rifles they had brought with them out of the bay, and was striding off up the shore with the men behind him.

Far too excited to sit still, Ted stood up in the stern of the small boat and watched the attack develop. The landing party was out of sight now. He could catch only an occasional glimpse of movement among the bushes as the sailors crept forward to surround the little clearing and the low, sprawling house. It was very quiet in the cove now. The wind rustled in the bayberry thickets, and a gray gull sailed over, mewing plaintively. Ted could hear his own heart pounding as he waited for the ominous rattle of gunfire to begin once more.

Still the minutes passed and still silence hung over the bay and the shore. At last Kelso's booming shout came back faintly from the edge of the clearing. He was telling the men in the shack to come out peaceably or take the consequences. There was no reply that Ted could hear, and the tense waiting began again.

Suddenly half a dozen of the attacking force jumped out of the bushes as if by a pre-arranged signal. They raced toward the shack and flung themselves down in the weeds at the base of the flimsy structure.

Like Ted, the two seamen in the skiff had been watching the clearing, and their craft had drifted closer without their noticing it. They were near enough now for the boy to see Bill Gates reach upward from where he lay on the ground and rip away several loose shingles. In a moment he had opened a ragged hole in the side of the house. There was a brief wait, then the lieutenant motioned to the seaman nearest him, and was handed the man's white sailor hat. He pulled a bunch of weeds, perched the hat on top of it and raised it slowly in front of the hole. Nothing happened.

After a few seconds Gates lowered the decoy head from the opening, got up calmly and walked straight to the door. His automatic was held ready as he kicked the door open, but he had no need to use it. Two men came stumbling out with their hands above their heads. The lieutenant stepped inside, took a quick look around and returned to the doorway.

"All right, boys," he called. "That's all there are. Tie 'em up!"

11

THE TWO PRISONERS WERE BIG, SUL-
len-looking men in seagoing clothes. When Bill
Gates undertook to question them in English, they
merely shrugged their shoulders. He switched to
brusque German then, and one of them gave him
short, unwilling answers.

"They're off the schooner," the lieutenant told
the Coast Guard men. "Claim they don't know
anything about the chaps that were here in the
house. Just fishermen, they say, and won't talk

about that gun they carried, aft. I think they'll give us a bit more information later, when we've taken 'em to Governors Island."

He turned to the ensign in charge of the cutter's landing party. "The schooner seems to be more in your line," he grinned. "If you'd like to search her you may find some interesting stuff. Meanwhile I'll see what's in the shack, here."

Ted had come ashore during the questioning of the prisoners, and when Gates went into the house again the boy accompanied him. The place was snug enough, inside. There were six bunks along the walls of the main room, besides comfortable chairs and a table on which playing cards lay scattered. The radio receiver still stood in the corner where Ted had heard it the night before. It was a compact model of foreign make, with a queer-looking antenna arrangement above it. There was no sign of a sending set, either there or in the back room which served as a kitchen.

"That gang that went out in the sedan must have taken their transmitter with 'em," Gates surmised.

"Their guns, too, I guess. Well, we'll know as soon as they hit the main road. That's too well patrolled for them to get away."

Ted was surprised at the neatness of the place. A big pile of dishes had been washed clean and stacked at the side of the sink. Even the dishcloth was carefully wrung out and hung to dry by the window.

The top of the cook-stove was still hot. Bill Gates lifted one of the lids and gave a whistle. "Burned their papers," he said. "But the fire didn't finish all of 'em. Let's see what we've got here."

With care he lifted out the still smoldering scraps and laid them on the kitchen table. There was a corner of a typewritten sheet with parts of several sentences unburned. The words were in German, and even the lieutenant's translation seemed to make no sense.

"It's probably code," he guessed. "I doubt if it would tell us anything we don't know, but our boys can have some fun deciphering it."

The largest piece of paper was part of a U. S.

Geodetic Survey map. As Gates studied it he became more interested. "Now we may be getting somewhere," he told Ted. "Here's Chatsworth, in the lower corner. If it was all here, the top would be up beyond Whitesbog, right along the Fort Dix line. And look here—close to the burned edge—they've marked a cross on this road beside the swamp! That's the very place where the truck unloaded provisions. Hang the luck! If another inch or two of paper hadn't burned, we might find out where that hideout of theirs was!"

He folded the scraps neatly and put them in his pocket. "We'll go exploring 'round there some day, Teddy," he grinned. "Right now and for a while to come I'm going to be mighty busy. These Fifth Column boys aren't quitting just because we've caught one gang. Well, it's time we were on our way."

As they were leaving the house they heard a sharp explosion and a startled yell. A Coast Guard sailor stood by the edge of the water staring at his right hand, bloody and mangled. A crowd of his mates surrounded him and Gates and the ensign shouldered their way through to his side.

"What happened, Reynolds?" snapped the blue-clad officer.

"It was a—a fountain-pen, sir," the sailor gasped. His face was chalky white. "I picked it up aboard the schooner—just for a souvenir, like. When I took the cap off—it—it blew up in my hand!"

"Crew of Number Two boat!" the ensign shouted. "Take Reynolds back to the cutter and get that wound dressed. Jackson, you know first aid. Get the kit out of the boat locker and do what you can for him on the way. Any of the rest of you men pick up any 'souvenirs'?"

A big, shambling seaman pulled a silver-colored cigarette case out of his pocket.

"I did, sir," he replied sheepishly. "I ain't opened it yet." And he held out the case.

"Put it down there in the sand, and stand away, you men." The ensign drew his big Navy revolver and took careful aim at the innocent-looking thing on the ground. As he pulled the trigger there was a double report—the crack of the gun and a louder explosion that followed on the instant.

Flying bits of metal flashed outward in a five-yard circle, barely missing some of the sailors' legs. The blast left a miniature bomb crater more than a foot deep in the sand.

Ted glanced at the two prisoners, standing under guard a short distance down the shore. One of them —the one who had refused to talk—had a sneering grin on his lips as he watched.

"All right, men," barked the ensign. "You've had a lesson. See you don't forget it. Man the boats, now, and lively."

He saluted Bill Gates and stepped into the stern sheets as his boat shoved off.

Back at the Cedar Beach station, Gates lost no time in telephoning headquarters. The news he received was good. Army Intelligence men and State Police had nabbed the gray sedan when it crossed the highway, and captured the six men in it before they could put up any resistance. There was also a sending set in the car. The lieutenant reported his own prisoners and asked that an Army truck be sent to carry them to Fort Dix.

At Kelso's invitation, he and Ted ate lunch with the Coast Guard men. Then they got into the convertible, said good-by to the kindly officer and set out for home.

The sun was hidden in a solid bank of clouds, blowing up from the east, as they rolled across the long bay bridge, and the air had a chill in it.

"Feels like rain coming on," Ted yawned. He was beginning to realize how little sleep he had had the night before.

"Yep," said the red-haired Army man. "That's what the weather report told us this morning. A good, smart rain—maybe a three-day northeaster. That'll settle the forest fire danger for a while and fill up the wells. Guess you won't mind that, will you?"

"Not me! I can think of a lot o' things more fun than hauling water in the wagon."

Ted was quiet for a few minutes. There was

something he wanted to say but he felt shy about it

"You've been mighty kind, letting me in on all this," he told Gates finally. "I don't s'pose I've got any business asking you, but one time you told me you had a book about birds you were going to lend me. I hoped you wouldn't forget, that's all."

"Well, by thunder!" the lieutenant exclaimed. "It clean slipped my mind in all the excitement. But I've got it for you—right here in the car. Here's the key to the glove compartment. Open it up."

What Ted found was a smallish book in a well-worn green cover. Inside, nearly every page had a colored illustration of a bird, with a description under it.

"Ever hear of Audubon, the naturalist?" Gates asked.

"Sure. One o' the teachers told us about him, at school."

"Well, those pictures are reproductions—pretty poor ones—of Audubon's bird paintings. They're the finest things of their kind ever done in this country—or the world, I guess. You can't get much idea of the originals from these cheap color plates, but at least they'll help a little in identifying the birds you see."

"Gosh," said Ted, turning the pages with respect. "I'll sure take good care o' this. I think the pictures are swell. Look at that blue jay—just as natural as if he was alive!"

They drove north on the shore highway to Barnegat, where the State Police were holding the men captured in the gray car. The sedan itself was standing in a sandy parking space beside the town hall. Around it a little crowd of people had gathered— clammers and fishermen in rubber boots, barefooted boys and aproned housewives. They were staring curiously at a bullet hole in one of the rear fenders and a blown-out tire.

Bill Gates took Ted inside the building and nodded to the State Police sergeant by the door. "I'd like to ask these fellows a few questions," he said. "But first I want the boy here to look 'em over."

The prisoners sat in a sullen row on a bench in one of the rear rooms. They were handcuffed in pairs and a couple of strapping troopers were standing guard over them. Ted looked quickly along the row. There were tall men, short men, young men and middle-aged men in the group, but he saw at a glance that the big, shock-headed fellow called Gus was not among them. He had never had a good look at Jake, the driver of the truck, so he couldn't tell about him till he heard their voices.

Gates began shooting questions at them. Some answered in English, one or two in German. One black-browed, scowling man in better clothes than the rest refused to speak at all at first. When he was finally persuaded to break silence he gave his name as Kurt Riesling.

Three of the men admitted having been on the schooner and said they had shipped as ordinary fishermen from a port in Nova Scotia. The others stoutly denied any knowledge of the Fort Dix forest fire, though they could give no satisfactory explanation for having visited the bayside shack.

Ted listened carefully as each man spoke. When the questioning was finished and he was outside again with Bill Gates, he shook his head.

"I know for sure that one of 'em isn't there," he told the lieutenant. "The other one—Jake, he was called—had a different voice from any o' those six. I'm afraid we didn't catch 'em all."

Gates frowned. "Well, it wouldn't be strange if a few got away," he answered. "I figured there were at least five in the gang on shore, and another five would be about the smallest crew that could sail the schooner. It's possible a couple of men are still hiding out in the woods. I'll tell the men to be on the lookout for 'em."

"There's one more thing," said Ted. "When I was in the truck I heard some talk about two men they called Kurt an' Johnny. Jake said he figured they'd got away all right an' would be waiting for 'em down here. One o' the prisoners said his name was Kurt Riesling. I sort o' thought he looked like the boss o' the gang."

"Yes," Gates nodded. "I picked him for the ringleader, too. It sounds as if he might have been the chap that was sending those code messages from back there in the swamp."

The first drops of rain began to fall as the car rolled northwestward through the Barrens. Soon it was a steady drizzle. Ted, still wearing the torn shirt and dungarees in which he had set out, began to shiver as the temperature dropped.

"Hey, kid!" his friend exclaimed. "That summer weather we've had is over. Put on my sweater, there in the back, and roll up the window."

By the time they turned off the highway into the wood road that led toward home, Ted was warm again. He was just beginning to realize that he was homesick. Never before in all his life had he spent a night away from Creature Comfort, and so much had happened in the last thirty hours that it seemed as if he had been gone a month.

He could hear Tramp's deep bark before they were in sight of the clearing, and he edged forward on the seat in his eagerness. As they came out of the pines he saw the gray old house and the little old man standing in the rain, peering anxiously from under his dripping hat brim.

Grandpa Winslow waited till the car stopped. Then he stumped forward, trying to hide the look of relief that had been on his face.

"Well!" he growled. "Durn near time you got home, young man! Gallivanting 'round the country without e'er a word to tell us where you been!"

He gave Gates an elaborate wink over Ted's shoulder as the boy jumped out.

The lieutenant refused his invitation to stop in for a cup of coffee. "I've got a lot of details to attend to, up at the Fort," he explained. "There'll be a long report to write about this day's work, and you can bet Ted's part in it will get plenty of mention. Don't be too rough on him, Mr. Winslow. He started to catch pneumonia on the way up here, so get some warm clothes on him."

He grinned, waved and put the car in gear. Even before he was out of the dooryard, Grandpa Winslow grabbed Ted by the arm.

"Get yourself inside, out o' this rain," he commanded. "There's a good fire in the kitchen, an' you'll find a clean flannel shirt an' a pair o' jeans on the chair."

The old man followed him in, and bustled about the stove while Ted was changing his clothes. "I reckon you could stand some good hot cocoa," he announced. "Now, then, start from the beginning, an' let's hear your story. I got the scare o' my life when ol' Doc came in the yard yesterday. Couldn't make out what had become o' you, but I reckoned you weren't hurt when I saw the lines hung up on the hames. Where in heck did you disappear to, anyhow?"

It took the boy a long time to tell his story, and the rainy afternoon was growing dark before he finished. "Well," he said at last, "that's about the whole of it. I feel fine now, an' I reckon it's time to get the chores done."

"Hmm," his grandfather grunted. "Sounds to me like you'd had all the excitement a boy could stand in one vacation. Think you'll be able to stay home now for a spell?"

"Oh, sure!" Ted laughed. "Don't worry, Gramps. You won't have to do any milking!" But as he went toward the barn he promised himself one more expedition before school started again. Now that he knew the way he meant to find out something more about the spies' former hiding-place in the swamp.

12

THE RAIN POURED STEADILY ALL THAT night. It was beating a soothing rhythm on the roof when Ted crawled into his bed under the eaves. Safe and snug and very sleepy, he thought he had never felt anything so comfortable in his life as those clean sheets.

Next morning when he woke, the rain was still coming down in gray torrents, slanting from the northeast. Ordinarily he would have been disgruntled at having a storm intrude on his holidays.

But when he thought of the dry wells and shrunken streams and fire-scorched woods he was grateful for every drop.

His grandfather, too, was in high spirits when Ted came downstairs. He was whistling "Hot Time in the Old Town"—always a good sign with him. After the barn work was done and the kitchen cleared up, he got his old brass fife from the closet and played it shrilly, giving a spirited rendition of "Goodbye, Dolly Gray" and "The Girl I Left Behind Me," hopping around the house in march time. The boy knew his story must have taken the old soldier back to Spanish War days.

"Talk about going ashore after the enemy in boats—" Grandpa Winslow exclaimed, sighting along his fife like the barrel of a carbine—"why, there was one time down there at Guantanamo—" And he was off again on a yarn that Ted had heard many times and knew by heart.

He listened with apparent attention, but the word "boats" had touched off an idea in his head. If he was going to do any real exploring in what he thought was "Hoquadunk Creek," he would need a boat of some kind. His grandfather had had one years ago, but Ted knew it had long since fallen apart. As he checked over the scattered neighbors in his mind, he remembered that the fire warden, Joe Lucas, owned an old canoe. If it didn't leak too much maybe he could borrow it.

The storm kept up through the day and when Ted went to the barn at five, he took a look at the well on the way. Lifting a plank beside the pump, he dropped a pebble and listened. The splash was quick and loud.

"Water's right up where it belongs," he reported on his return.

"Well, that's a help," the old man replied. "This rain isn't likely to keep up much longer. Most o' the prickliness has gone out o' my late-lamented foot."

Ted looked at the dark, wet window-pane where the lances of the rain seemed to be driving harder than ever. But he had lived with his grandfather too long to doubt any weather prediction he made.

"If it's clear by morning," he said, "d'you s'pose you'll be needing the horse an' wagon?"

The old man shot him a keen glance. "Don't know's I will," he answered. "You got use for 'em?"

Ted tried to make his reply sound offhand, but it was hard to do under that sharp-eyed appraisal. "Yeah," he said. "There's something I thought I'd like to borrow from Joe Lucas."

"Hmm. Well, see to it anything you borrow gets good care, an' return it soon as you can," his grand-father advised. He didn't ply the boy with questions —just let it go at that.

Sure enough, the downpour ended before day-light next morning. When Ted put his tousled head out the window the air was clear and fresh and fragrant of the wet woods.

He raced through the chores and went on foot to Joe Lucas' house, which stood in a clearing on a little sand road, two miles to the south. As he expected, the warden was still at home. Right after a heavy rain there was no danger of forest fire, and Lucas was setting out tomato plants in the little garden plot behind his barn.

"Well, Teddy!" the big man chuckled. "How's it feel to be the biggest hero in two counties?"

The boy got red. "Heck," he said, "who called me anything like that? I was so scared my knees kept shaking most o' the time."

"That don't signify a thing," replied the warden. "There was a whole battalion of us felt the same way at Château-Thierry. But we were loadin' an' firin' so fast the Jerries never knew it. I saw Bill Gates yesterday an' he seems right proud o' you."

Pleased, but uncomfortable, Ted changed the subject. "Joe," he said, "could you spare that canoe o' yours for a day?"

"Sure. I ain't used her in two years, though. You'll prob'ly find her in pretty bad shape. She's layin' right back there by the creek. Just take the path yonder. It's only a step."

Ted followed the path a hundred yards through the pines and reached the creek bank. The canoe looked somewhat discouraging at first glance. Weatherbeaten and long unpainted, it was turned keel up across a couple of logs. There were places where the bottom had been torn by snags and crudely patched. And part of the metal guard was gone from the bow end, leaving the ragged edges of the canvas and a hole that let daylight through. When he turned the craft over he found the ribs and cedar planking were sound. There was a paddle, with the edge of the blade split off, tucked under the battered stern thwart.

"I reckon I can fix her up," he told Lucas, as he returned through the clearing.

"Good. Keep her as long as you want," the warden answered. "You aimin' to take a trip?"

"Yeah, just exploring 'round a little on one o' the creeks," said Ted, casually. He didn't like to give his secret away until he had found something worth talking about.

It was still early in the forenoon when he got back to Creature Comfort. He rummaged around in the shed where his grandfather's little forge stood, and eventually found the things he needed—an old pot of hardened, black pitch and a strip of stout canvas.

Then he harnessed Doc to the wagon and drove back to Lucas' house. The warden had driven off to the tower by that time, but Ted hitched the horse in the dooryard and took his patching materials down to the creek.

Dry wood was hard to find, but he cut some resinous slivers out of the bole of a dead pine and got a small fire going in a sandy, open space. When it was burning well he hung the iron pitch-pot in the flames and cut his canvas to overlap the broken stem of the canoe.

The sun had already dried out the craft's bottom, and in a few minutes the pitch was soft enough to use. Ted whittled out a stick to make a small, flat spatula. With this implement he began smearing a thick layer of pitch into the hole in the bow and along its sides. Then he applied the canvas, pressing it tightly into place. And finally he gave the whole patch an outer coating of the sticky, black substance from the pot.

It was not a neat or handsome job but it looked as if it would keep the water out. Ted took the pitch and the paddle back to the wagon, then returned to the creek, crawled in under the canoe and struggled to his feet with the ribbed bottom supported on his back and shoulders. He had never had much experience with canoes but he figured that was the only way he could carry it. Fortunately, the trees along the path were far enough apart to let him through with his load. He was pretty tired when he got to the clearing but it was easier to keep going than to put the burden down and then shoulder it again.

At last he staggered up to the tail of the wagon and set the forward end of the canoe on it. After he had caught his breath he heaved it up the rest of the way. It was a relief to get that much of the job done, for it was the only part of his plan that had worried him.

With the canoe securely on the wagon bed, he drove out along the sand road and southward through the woods to the highway. There was little motor traffic that morning, but Ted didn't use the concrete. He let old Doc plod along on the gravel at the right of the roadway.

He had figured out in his own mind just about where the highway must cross his mysterious creek. For half a mile he watched the roadside for a bridge or culvert, and even when he reached the place he almost failed to see it. The highway was raised on a gravel fill, several feet above the wilderness that reached away on either hand. Thick brush and bushy pine tops crowded up to the embankment and there was no concrete bridge wall to mark the crossing. Leaning over the right side of the wagon seat, Ted happened to notice a spot where the steep slope of the bank was hidden by cedars. He stopped the horse and went to look, for he knew that cedars usually meant water. Sure enough, when he scrambled down the bank he found the arch of a huge corrugated iron culvert and a swiftly flowing stream of muddy water, half hidden by the thicket. The ground below was swampy, and he could see where the channel twisted southward among the cedars.

Ted had some doubts then, for it didn't appear to be much of a creek. Still, there was no other possible place that could serve as an outlet for his swampy pond, and there was a lot of water coming through the arch. Maybe the stream would broaden out if he followed it farther down.

There were no cars in sight when he wrestled the canoe off the wagon and down the bank. He had to bend the bushes apart with his elbows and drag the boat through to the water. At the edge of the stream he tipped the gunwale under until there were three or four inches of water in the canoe. It seemed a good idea to let the dry, old planking soak overnight before starting his voyage. Then he wedged the bow firmly between the trunks of two cedars, so that the craft couldn't drift away, and climbed back to the road. Looking down from the wagon it was impossible to see any part of the canoe. Ted was well satisfied with his forenoon's work.

He drove home and unharnessed in time for dinner. Grandpa Winslow made no comment on his morning's expedition, and they spent the rest of the day working together, mending fence along the north line.

"If you won't be needing me tomorrow, Gramps,"

the boy said at suppertime, "I thought I'd go off in the woods. I'm taking along that book about birds," he added with a slightly guilty feeling. "The one Bill Gates loaned me. I want to learn some more kinds so I can tell 'em when I see 'em."

It wasn't a lie, he assured himself. He really did intend to carry the book and use it. But there was a look in his grandfather's wise blue eyes that made him wonder if the old man hadn't seen through his story. He could still make a clean breast of it, and for a moment he was on the verge of doing so— until he thought how silly he would look if the swamp should turn out to be a false lead after all. Besides, it would be more fun to surprise everybody if he should find something.

Ted studied the bird book by lamplight till nine o'clock and then went to bed. He was up with the call of the first song sparrow next morning, eager to get started. Fortunately it was another glorious spring day. The air had been much cooler since the rain, and the woods had now had time to dry out, so that he could walk without bringing down a shower on himself every time he shook a branch.

By seven-thirty he had finished his morning tasks, eaten breakfast and packed up one of his usual sandwich lunches.

"Come on, Tramp," he called. "It'll do you good to stretch your legs."

The big dog needed no second invitation. He came tearing across the yard like a black thunderbolt, jumped high enough to give his master's cheek a flick of the tongue in passing, and dashed ahead to the edge of the woods. Once there he waited, tail wagging, to see which direction they would take.

Ted cut south through the pines, making almost a bee-line for the highway. He went fast, guided by old blazes he had made years before, and in a little more than an hour the broad, white road was in sight. The route he had taken skirted the swampy ground, so that they reached the highway some distance above the stream.

On the gravel shoulder they turned left. The boy kept Tramp close at his side and held his collar every time a car passed. When they came to the culvert he took a quick glance up and down the road, then plunged down the bank into the brush.

The canoe was just as he had left it. With a little tugging he got it out from between the cedar trunks and dragged it ashore to tip out the water. The pitch around the bow had hardened solid and tight. Ted had a proud moment when he launched the craft again and took his place in the stern. The book and the lunch parcel were laid carefully on a pile of twigs in front of his feet, for he didn't entirely trust the leak-proof qualities of his patch. He took the paddle and told Tramp to get in. For a moment the dog hesitated, then leaped into the middle of the canoe with a crash that nearly upset it. At last they were off.

The first part of that morning's cruise was a good deal harder work than Ted had expected. The art of steering a canoe was something he had to learn by trial and error, and the course of the stream was so narrow and twisting that even an expert would have been in difficulties.

In places there seemed to be no channel at all, but

simply a dark sweep of water running through dense cedar clumps. Time after time he got out and waded, hunting a passage wide enough to drag the canoe through. Often he ran on sunken logs and had to pull his craft off. And more than once it was necessary to carry around some impassable obstacle. At the end of two hours he doubted if he had gone half a mile.

After that it grew easier. The stream was deeper and wider and the current ran less swiftly. Ted was beginning to get the hang of his paddling, too. His principal trouble now was Tramp. The dog had been in and out of the boat so often during the earlier stages of the journey that he had no wish to lie quietly amidships. He was constantly crowding to one side or the other, sniffing and staring at things along the bank. And every time he shifted his weight the canoe tipped perilously.

Ted lost patience with him at last and put him ashore. "Go on home, Tramp," he commanded roughly. "You're just a nuisance, an' I wish to thunder I hadn't brought you. You hear me? Git!"

That was an order the dog understood. His tail drooped and he hung his head, contriving to look so ashamed and so reproachful that Ted almost weakened. He waited for a minute, then, with a final "Home, Tramp!", he turned his back resolutely and paddled away down the creek.

13

THE OPEN REACHES OF WATER ENDED
before Ted had gone far. Once again he found himself in a shadowy jungle of cedar growth, where the
stream coiled and twisted like a snake. Sometimes
he was wholly lost in a maze of tortuous false chan-
nels, only to discover after long minutes that the
current was running in a different direction from
the way he was trying to go.

It was while he was getting his bearings after
such an experience that he noticed higher ground

on his left. Between the cedar branches he could see a bank of red-streaked sand rising from the water, and the leaves of scrub oaks rustling above it.

He swung the bow over with a twist of his wrist, and drove the canoe in on a narrow, sandy beach. It was a pleasant thing to stand on firm ground again. He pulled the light craft up till most of its length was hidden in a clump of blueberry bushes. The book and the little bundle of sandwiches had remained comparatively dry through the hazards of the voyage and he carried them with him as he turned to climb the bank.

Thrusting through the sand were ribs of what appeared to be crumbly, dark-red stone, rough and hard to the soles of his bare feet. He broke off a fragment and looked at it more closely. It was bog iron! All around him he saw lumps and masses of the stuff—more of it than he had ever found in one place before.

With growing excitement, he pushed his way between the oaks and crossed a narrow ridge. On the other side the ground sloped off again into dark

water and cedar thicket. He was on an island, hidden there in the middle of an unexplored swamp!

Overhead, the sun showed him it was past noon,
and he realized that he had been hungry for some
time. Hastily he unwrapped the parcel and attacked
his food, eager to finish and find out more about
this place. Finding the iron had raised his hopes,
for he was sure it had been brought there by human
hands. That could mean only one thing—an iron
works. Ted had heard enough about the old-time
furnaces to know that bog ore was usually dug out
of low, swampy places where the water had depos-
ited it for centuries. He figured it would then be
piled up somewhere near the furnace, ready for
smelting as it was needed. That was the only way
he could account for such a quantity of ore on a
sandy slope several feet above the water.

Munching away at the sandwiches, he came on
the extra one he had put in for Tramp, and felt a
twinge of regret about having sent him home. Not
that he doubted the dog could find the way, but
there was the highway to cross. Still, he comforted

himself, Tramp had pretty good sense for a back-woods dog. He was probably nearly home by this time.

Ted was in the act of wrapping up the last sandwich and stuffing it in his pocket when a bird chirped softly in the tree above his head. Looking up he saw a flash as vivid as a flame among the oak leaves. He held his breath, waiting for that brilliant spot of scarlet to appear again, but the bird seemed to have vanished completely. After a moment a cheerful song came to him from another tree, thirty or forty yards away. The song was a little like a robin's, he thought, but with a different trill. He gripped the little green book and tiptoed toward the sound, sure that it was the strange red bird singing. As he drew close he caught another glimpse—a better one this time. The songster perched in full view for four or five seconds before it darted away.

The boy thumbed hastily through the pages of the book. When he came to it he knew there could be no mistake. There was the picture—bright scarlet all over except for the black wings and tail. The name under it was "Scarlet Tanager."

Keeping the place with his finger, Ted hurried on, eager for still another sight of the bird. He had gone perhaps a hundred yards along the wooded ridge when he found his way blocked by a queer-shaped mound, covered with a tangle of wild grape-vines. He started to push his way around it through the undergrowth when something turned under his foot. He stooped and picked it up. It was the broken half of a brick, old and weathered, and when he looked more closely at the ground he saw others— dozens of them, buried under the leaves and creep-ers.

Ted turned quickly, studying the tall, conical mound, and gave a gasp of delight. The whole thing was built of bricks, loose and tumbling now, but still preserving the outline of a furnace!

He forgot all about the tanager in the excitement of his discovery. Shoving the book inside his shirt to get it out of the way, he went scrambling up the side of the pile, clinging to the tough grapevine strands and digging his toes into crannies between the bricks.

The top stood fifteen or twenty feet above the ground. He leaned over the crumbling, smoke-blackened edge and peered down into the open center, where charcoal had once burned the slag out of bog iron ore. Half filled now with bricks and leaf mold, it was a disappointment to Ted, for he had expected the cavity to be dark and mysterious, like a well. But thrusting up out of the mass of rubble was something that revived his interest. It was part of a huge band of black, pitted iron. Half an inch thick and six or seven inches broad, it might have been the hoop that originally bound the top of the furnace.

Ted jumped down into the hollow and fingered the uneven surface of the hand-forged metal. It wasn't rusty. He had heard about the durability of the old Jersey iron and here was abundant proof. This piece must have been exposed to the weather for a hundred years. Thinking he saw a crack, low down near its base, he leaned closer and gave a startled exclamation. It was a letter "C," stamped deep in the surface and still quite legible. Quickly the boy pulled up the bricks around it and flung them aside. More letters came to light as the iron was laid bare. "C-L-A-S-S-O-N," he read. Classon! The name on the old deed in Mt. Holly Court House!

He stood up, panting, and fairly danced for joy. There was no longer any question about it. He had found Bill Gates' "Lost Forge."

The thrill of discovery had gripped Ted now and he had no thought of turning back till he had thoroughly explored the place. Beyond the furnace the high ground sloped down to cedar swamp again. He might have thought this was the end of the island if he had not found traces of an old road leading straight into the bog. As he walked along it he felt the round, firm outlines of logs under his feet. It was a corduroy wagon track, still solid in spite of the years it had been buried there in the muck.

Even before Ted entered the shadow of the cedars, a cloud had crept over the sun. The birds stopped singing and in the silence the swamp seemed to wait for him, still and dark and threatening. The farther he went along the ancient road, the lower fell his spirits. Perhaps it was the damp, chill air that sent a shiver down his spine, or perhaps some instinct, deep in his bones, was warning him of danger. He shook off the feeling angrily, and tried to whistle, but the sound faltered and died on his lips.

At last he saw the end of the corduroy and rising ground beyond. The cedars gave way to sweet gums and blackjack oaks. He drew a long breath of relief and hurried onward, following the sandy, moss-grown patches that marked the track of the old road.

He had gone another hundred yards when a faint, sweet perfume stopped him in his tracks. It wasn't a woods smell. It made him think of farmhouses and country dooryards. Pushing his way through the thicket a few steps to his right, he came on a huge, straggly lilac bush. It looked more like a tree, but the neat, heart-shaped leaves and scattered sprays of purple blossoms left no doubt. How did it come there, alone and forlorn in the wilderness? He knew the answer. Where there were lilacs there must once have been a house!

Looking at the ground as he cast about for some sign of an old cellar-hole, Ted did not see the building till he was almost in its shadow. When he glanced up he was so startled that for a long moment he could only stand and stare. Half hidden by the close-growing trees and strands of creeper, its bulk rose big and dark out of the undergrowth.

The house was old—very old, Ted thought—but its size bespoke the builder's pride. Abandoned to the weather for generations, it still looked staunch and dignified. It was two full stories high, and the end facing him was broad enough for four windows. The wide cedar clapboards were warped and gray and the moldy, curling shingles gave the roof a shaggy look, but there was no sag in the line of the ridge-pole.

Ted went past the corner of the old mansion on tiptoe, as if half afraid he might wake it from its long sleep. Brush grew thick against the sightless windows and some of their small panes were broken. As he approached what must have been the front entrance he saw the scattered remnants of a brick walk, long since uprooted by good-sized trees. A big, bushy pine had shouldered roughly into the doorway, but through its branches the boy could see the arch of a fine fanlight and the black outline of an iron knocker.

He made his way among the bushes to the step and tried the heavy latch. It refused to lift, and the door itself stood firm against his strongest push. There was nothing for it but to continue his circuit of the house.

At the southern end he saw a huge, brick chimney jutting from the roof. Part of its top had tumbled in but the massive base stood solid and strong. Ted would not have given the chimney a second glance if he had not happened to notice a slim, dark line rising out of it. He stopped and looked again. It was a length of steel tubing that shot straight up to a height of forty feet above the roof. Taut wire guys held it erect, and from an insulator at its top four parallel wires slanted off to a tree a hundred feet away. From a plane, flying over the Barrens,

Ted knew the antenna would be invisible. And looking at the gray-green, lichen-covered shingles he could understand why the house itself had escaped detection. Nature had given it a camouflage that would blend almost perfectly with the surrounding foliage.

What a report he could make to Bill Gates now! Ted had all the proof he needed that the mysterious radio signals used by the spy ring had come from this very spot—the "Lost Forge" of Jared Classon!

He was still grinning with satisfaction at this discovery when he came around the southwest corner of the old house. Clawing his way through a tangle of bushes he suddenly found himself in a neatly cleared space, so utterly different that it gave him a momentary shock. The undergrowth had been cut away from around the back doorstep and the door itself stood partly open. A recently used path led down the slope to the creek bank on the west.

After the first startled instant Ted laughed at himself. He should have expected something like this after seeing the radio antenna. The men who had stayed here would naturally have tried to make the place livable.

He crossed the little open glade under the trees and hesitated before mounting the step to the back door. Except for the soft stirring of a breeze in the pine tops, silence lay heavy over the island. Lonely cloud shadows drifted across the woods, and no birds sang. Once again the boy felt that tingle of impending danger that he had known in the swamp.

It took real resolution to cross the threshold of the strange old dwelling, but once inside Ted breathed more easily. He was in a big, old-fashioned kitchen, well lighted by three rear windows. There was an iron sink with a hand pump, a scarred old table and three plain kitchen chairs. Backed up to the brick-work of the chimney was a huge, antique cook-stove, littered with the dust of years. But in addition to these articles that obviously belonged to a past generation, the room contained a modern gasoline camp stove and two folding cots, with the disordered bedding still on them.

The floor of broad, uneven pine boards had been

swept within a few days and except for the corner where the old stove stood the room was fairly clean.

Ted crossed to the sink and worked the pump handle up and down. It creaked a little but to his surprise water flowed from the spout after three or four strokes. He filled a battered tin dipper that stood by the sink and tasted the water warily. It was clear and cold and sweet. Evidently the recent tenants had put the well in working order. Thirstily the boy drank and drank again before he turned to continue his exploration.

There was little more in the kitchen to occupy his attention. He saw a big tin box under the table and when he lifted the lid he found two wrapped loaves of baker's bread, doubtless a week old and stale by now. A dozen new cans of tomatoes and fruit stood in a dusty cupboard among ancient pots and pans. The spies must have lived pretty comfortably during their stay, he thought.

In the wall of the room opposite the windows another door stood ajar. It looked as if it might lead into the middle part of the house and Ted pushed it open, peering into a dark, musty-smelling butler's pantry. Gingerly he tiptoed through it to a second door and lifted the latch. The sight he saw as the door creaked open made his eyes pop wide. He was in a big, square room, filled with massive mahogany furniture—a dining-table, a huge sideboard, a china-closet and a dozen chairs of heavy, carved wood. Over them all lay the dust of many years, but the afternoon light that streamed through the south windows glinted on fine porcelain and glass and tarnished silver.

Awed by such magnificence, he reached out a shaking hand and touched a great silver candlestick on the sideboard. The dust fell from it like soft flakes of snow, and the metal beneath was darkened and dull, but there was no concealing the lovely workmanship. Lifting it gently he was amazed to find it weighed three or four pounds. That was only one of a dozen splendid silver pieces in the room. And there were other things, the value of which he could only guess—an immense crystal chandelier hanging above the table—beautiful wall paneling and carved lintels above the doors—a dim portrait of a woman in an ornate gilded frame.

It required a certain amount of imagination to see that gracious room as it might have looked a hundred years before, but Ted had a picture of it in his mind. Candles burning softly in the chandelier and on the sideboard. Stately men and smiling ladies in evening dress. The rich iron-master astonishing his city friends with the hospitality of a wilderness mansion.

For a moment or two the boy stood bemused, his thoughts far back in that heyday of the Pine Barrens forges. Then he went toward a door on his left which stood partially open. He had almost reached the threshold when a sound made him halt in sudden fear.

A thud of heavy feet at the back entrance—then in the kitchen itself. And a voice that made Ted's heart sink: "I'll clean the fish, Jake. You git the stove goin'. Say—who left that door open?"

14

TED'S MEMORY OF THAT VOICE WAS
too recent and too unpleasant for him to be mistaken.
It was the big, shock-headed man called Gus, and
his truck-driver confederate was with him!

At any instant the boy expected one of them to
come in through the pantry looking for a possible
intruder. Shaking with fright he tried to remember
whether he had left any evidence of his presence in
the kitchen. He thought not, but he couldn't be
sure. In the dining-room the tracks of his bare feet

were sickeningly plain, and it was too late now to try to obliterate them.

How was he to get out? A glance at the windows discouraged any hope in that direction. Unopened for countless years, and choked with vines, they would have to be smashed before anybody could escape through them. The one possibility that he could see was the door at his elbow. He pushed it gently, an inch at a time, praying under his breath that its hinges would give no betraying squeak. When the opening was wide enough to admit his body, he slipped through and stood in a spacious hallway that filled the center of the house. The only light came through the door by which he had just entered and down the winding stairway from an unseen window on the upper floor.

Cautiously he went toward the front door, stepping in deep dust and the crumbling remnants of fallen plaster. The huge iron bolt would not move when he tugged at it, and he was afraid to use any noisier means of opening it.

Desperation gripped the boy's heart then. He

knew how an animal must feel, trapped and cornered by the dogs. Looking about him wildly he saw the broad curve of the staircase. Some of the steps were gone, and part of the heavy banister rail had fallen across it, making a rough barricade. He hurried to the stairs with an idea of climbing over the obstruction, but as he trod on the lowest step it cracked ominously under his foot. Holding his breath in terror, he waited for the spies to come and find him. As the seconds passed it appeared that they had not heard. They were still moving about in the kitchen, preparing their meal.

Ted did not dare try the ascent again. He crept along the narrower part of the hall to the darkest place he could find, and crouched there in a corner behind the staircase. The only plan he could think of now was to wait until the two men went out again as they had done that afternoon.

Occasionally he could hear their voices, coming in gruff monosyllables from the kitchen. After a while such light as there was began to grow even dimmer. It must be past sunset, he thought. He heard a faint sputter of something frying, and after that a pleasant smell stole through the old house. They were cooking fish for supper.

It was almost wholly dark now in the hallway. One of Ted's legs had gone to sleep, and as he shifted his weight he felt something move behind his shoulder, where it rested against the wall. He put out an exploring hand. What he had thought was a panel in the woodwork turned out to be a low, square door, opening into a sort of cupboard under the stairs.

Surprisingly enough, the door made no noise as he pulled it farther open. It was very loose on its hinges and he was afraid for a moment that the screws would let go of the rotted wood and it would drop off under his hand.

He crept into the closet and pulled the door as nearly tight as possible behind him. In the utter blackness he could feel several hard objects on the floor, but there was room to lie curled up in reasonable comfort. Dust, undisturbed for ages, rose around him and filtered into his nostrils. He made a futile grab at his nose but it was too late. The sneeze came quick and sharp—*ker-choo!*

"Hey, what was that?" asked Gus, in the kitchen. The partition must have been thin between the closet and the pantry, for the voice was almost as distinct as if he had been in the same room.

A chair scraped on the kitchen floor and heavy feet clumped through into the dining-room. "Sounded like somebody sneezed," the big man said.

Ted could hear him blundering around among the chairs, peering into corners in the dusk. Then the steps came on through the doorway into the hall, and for long seconds Gus stood there, listening.

The boy had an agonizing desire to sneeze again but he succeeded in strangling it, pressing his knuckles fiercely against his upper lip.

"Huh!" Gus muttered at last. "Durn funny thing." And he went back to the kitchen, still grumbling.

Ted heard Jake's deep chuckle. "You vorry some more, Gus? Dere's blenty noises in a old house. Der beams shnap und der vind rattles der doors."

"Yeah, I know, but this was different. You'd ha' heard it if you hadn't been chawin' on that crust o' bread. Only thing could make that kind o' noise would be an animal. Mebbe a rat or an owl—there's some o' them up in the attic, I reckon."

The men must have a light in the kitchen, Ted thought. They finished their meal and began cleaning up at the sink. There was a sound of pumping water, then the clink of plates and cutlery. Scraps of conversation came through the partition to the listening boy.

"How much longer you figger we've got to hang 'round here, Jake?"

"Oh, anodder veek, I t'ink."

"Ho hum! I'm sick o' the place right now. Still, you're prob'ly right. They'll quit huntin' us by that time. Tell you one thing, though. When I go I aim to be carryin' some silver along with me. There's too much good stuff in this house to leave it lay here."

"Ya—und dot's a goot vay to get shot!" Jake replied drily. "Ve got to travel light und fast."

"I dunno. It shouldn't be so tough. Can't be more'n twelve or fifteen mile to the railroad, an' we go along that till we hit a station. Let on we're a couple o' charcoal-burners goin' to town fer a spree. They've got no description of us, an' they're more apt to be watchin' the highways than a jerkwater railroad line like this. What'll be our move when we git to New York, Jake?"

"Chust you vait, Gus. I show you."

"No, but suppose we had to run fer it an' got separated. I ought to have some idea where to head."

"You valk a liddle vest from Broadvay on twenty-sevent'," Jake explained. "Vatch for a sign on der vinder, t'ree floors up—'Stossberg, Importer.' Dot's vere to go."

"Yeah, but they don't know me up there. Kurt hired me, an' it looks like he got caught."

"Vell, you knock on der door—t'ree times, like dis." There were three quick raps in the kitchen. "Den a feller dressed like vorkman opens und looks at you. 'Nobody here,' he says. 'I'm chust makin' repairs.' Und you say, 'I come from Hoboken.' 'Vat part of Hoboken?' he says, und you say 'Munich Gartens.' Dot's all dere is. Der feller lets you in, und in der back room is der boss."

"Okay, Jake. I can remember that much, I guess. An' I'll most likely be with you anyhow. Let's play some pinochle."

Ted heard chairs pulled up to the table and the faint rustling of shuffled cards. After that the conversation was about the game and couched in terms he didn't understand. Instead of listening he concentrated on memorizing the directions Jake had given his partner. If he ever got out of this predicament he knew Bill Gates could make good use of such information.

The boy dozed after a while, in spite of his cramped position. He had no idea what time it was when he woke again, but the card game must have ended, for he could hear a steady snoring on the other side of the thin wall.

Moving very slowly, so as not to raise another

cloud of dust in the closet, Ted inched the door open and crawled out. He had to feel his way along the side of the stairway and into the wider part of the hall, testing every floor board with his bare toes before he put his weight on it.

At the dining-room door he waited, holding his breath. The sounds continued, and he was sure he heard two different snores, one coming a little more quickly than the other. His eyes, used to the dark now, could pick out the various pieces of furniture dimly outlined by starlight from the windows.

He steadied himself by the door frame and moved forward again, tiptoeing slowly across the treacherous floor. He was just inside the pantry, when one of the men stopped snoring and gave a sort of choking cough. At that very moment a board creaked under Ted's foot. He drew back in terror, sure that the sound had been loud enough to rouse any but a heavy sleeper.

There was a harsh squeak from the springs of a cot in the kitchen, and Ted could almost see the wakened man sitting up to listen. He hardly dared to breathe as he stood there trembling in the dark. It was no use. His plan of escaping through the kitchen while they slept was doomed to failure, and the best he could hope for now was to get back to the closet under the stairs.

As he started his stealthy retreat, however, he remembered the footprints he had left in the dust. If either of the men entered the room in daylight they would certainly notice the tracks. In a flash of inspiration, Ted pulled off his shirt. He backed silently across the dining-room, swishing the garment to and fro, close to the floor. That ought to do some good, he figured, for he could feel the swirls of dust rising and settling around his toes.

Still swinging the shirt, he retraced his steps through the hall and reached the cubbyhole behind the staircase without hearing any further alarming noises. Once back in his hiding-place he could breathe more freely.

The snores in the adjoining room settled into their old rhythm and Ted decided to get some rest if he could. He put his shirt on again, then snuggled down with his head on his arm and tried to sleep. It took a long time. There were heavy periods of silence, broken by eerie rustlings and sudden snappings in the timbers of the wall. The boy found himself waiting for them with tense nerves, and it was only by an effort of will that he made himself relax.

After that he must have drifted off, for the next time he woke it was morning. A faint, gray light seeped in around the loosely hung door and there were sounds of movement in the kitchen. He concluded that Gus and Jake were just out of bed. They had nothing to say to each other beyond an occasional growling word, but the clink of pans sounded like breakfast.

Ted sat up painfully and stretched to get the kinks out of his cramped muscles. As the scent of frying bacon stole through the house, a sharp pang of hunger reminded him that he had had nothing to eat since his cold lunch of the day before. He got the leftover sandwich out of his pocket and ate it as quietly as he could.

It was hard to sit there without moving while his enemies yawned and loafed in the kitchen, but he controlled himself, hoping that sooner or later the men would leave the house.

An hour dragged by and at last the sounds of dish-washing ceased. Ted smelled the smoke of rank, strong tobacco in a pipe. Then the back door was opened and they went clumping out.

The boy curbed his eagerness while he counted slowly to a hundred, then pushed the door open and crept out of the closet. At the entrance to the dining-room and again in the pantry he waited, listening, before tiptoeing on. When he finally reached the kitchen the outer door was ajar and he could hear a faint sound of voices coming from some distance away. He judged the men were down at the creek bank.

There was a pitcher, half full of water, standing beside the sink. He didn't know how fresh the water was, but since he hardly dared to use the pump he put the rim of the pitcher to his lips and drank long and deep. Then he looked around for food. There was nothing left on the table, so he opened the big tin box and took three slices of bread from one of the wrapped loaves which had already been opened. It was dry but not moldy.

In the cupboard with the canned goods he found a partially filled jar of peanut butter. That was a real discovery. He would have something to spread on his bread. With both hands full of food, he pushed the cupboard door shut with his elbow and hurried to make his escape.

Ted was within a step of the back door and reaching forward to open it when he heard Gus and Jake coming into the clearing. Their voices sounded so close that the boy's heart skipped a beat. He darted back to the pantry and through the room beyond. At the door into the hall he turned and looked at the floor, thankful to see that his footprints were no more than smears on the dusty surface. Then, as the booted feet came noisily into the house, he stole along the hall and re-entered his dark little cubbyhole.

15

TED LEFT THE LOW DOOR AN INCH OR
two open so that he wouldn't suffocate. A little
light came in through the crack and he saw the
bread and peanut butter still in his hands as he
squatted there on the closet floor. He was too hungry to wait. Even with the sound of footsteps loud
on the other side of the partition, he stuffed his
mouth with bread. It tasted good in spite of its dry-
ness. Opening his jack-knife, he quietly removed
the cover from the jar and spread peanut butter

thickly over the remaining slices.

While he munched his meal, he could hear the men in the kitchen moving about restlessly.

"Hey," growled Jake. "Vat you do mit der peanut butter, huh? It aind't on der shelf."

"Sure it is," Gus answered with a yawn. "Look some more, you dumb Dutchman. Prob'ly right under your nose."

Ted nearly choked on the last mouthful. He pulled the door as tight as it would go and sat there in the darkness, waiting for developments. But it appeared his fright was groundless. After a few grumbling remarks Jake gave up the search and went back to the table.

Gus yawned again, even more loudly. "Not a thing to do in this stinkin' hole," he complained. "Haven't even got a magazine to look at. If we got to stay cooped up here I wish we still had the radio. Come on—I'll play you another game o' cards."

The noise of shuffling and the slap of the pasteboards on the table were the only sounds Ted heard for a while. He opened the door again and began looking around him to see if there was any way of making the closet more comfortable. He was curious also about the things he had felt with his hands but had been unable to identify.

The place extended back under the stairs for a distance of a good ten feet, and odds and ends were piled there in confusion.

Among the first things he found was an old pair of leather boots, crusted with green mold and gnawed by the small teeth of rodents—mice or squirrels, most likely. Beyond the boots was a sheet-iron lantern with a cone-shaped top and a ring for a handle. It was pierced with hundreds of nail holes for the light of the candle to shine through. As he expected, the socket was empty. A tallow dip was far too tasty a morsel for the wood mice to leave.

Next he came on a small, square iron receptacle with a hinged cover and a handle like that of a bucket. It took him a few minutes to figure out what it was, but some dusty fragments of charcoal at the bottom of the iron box gave him a clue. He had heard his grandfather talk about the old-fashioned foot-warmers and foot-stoves, and he decided this must be one of them. A shovelful of glowing coals would give heat for hours in such a contrivance.

There was an ancient scarf of fine figured silk that fell apart in feathery shreds when he tried to pick it up. And there was a pair of quaint old skates, made for the feet of a small child. They had wooden frames with slots in them through which crumbling leather straps passed, and the blades were of black iron, hand-forged, with a high curl over the toe. Ted wondered what had become of the little boy who once wore them. He could imagine him, rosy-cheeked, whizzing down the frozen creek with the skates buckled on over his copper-toed boots and a long wool muffler flying out behind him.

Feeling around in a dusty corner, Ted found a heavy iron door-stopper, cast in the form of a round-bellied British soldier, complete even to the cross-belts, gaiters and funny, high-pointed grenadier cap. He recognized the caricature from pictures of Bunker Hill and Yorktown that he had seen in his history books. It must have been made in the years following the Revolution, when the memory of red-coat troops was still fresh in Jersey households.

Beside the squat, iron figure, half-buried in the dust, was a little brass key. Ted picked it up and studied its shape. It was too small for a door key, but it might fit the lock of a china cupboard or a secretary. He slipped it into his pocket and peered about in the half darkness looking for still other treasures.

It seemed that he had finally exhausted the resources of the closet. There were no more objects of interesting shape. Only at the extreme end, right under the lower treads of the stairs, there was a sort of platform, raised seven or eight inches from the floor. He tried to figure why it should be there and crawled closer, running his hand idly along the side nearest to him. His fingers touched cold metal under the dust. The light was too dim to show him what it was, but he could feel the outline of a raised metal plate with an irregular shaped hole in the middle of it. A lock with a keyhole!

The thing wasn't a platform at all, but a low wooden box, nearly as wide as the stairs themselves. He felt the line of separation between the side and the top and made an effort to lift the lid. It rose a tiny fraction of an inch before it was stopped by the solid resistance of metal. The box was locked.

Ted's curiosity was aroused now. He leaned down and blew the dust away from the keyhole, got the brass key out of his pocket and tried it gently in the lock. Not only did it fit the hole but when he turned it the tumblers of the lock moved with a muffled click!

Before he attempted to raise the cover again, Ted sat still, waiting for his hands to steady themselves. Excited as he was about the possible contents of the chest, he didn't want to make a noise and be discovered. The sounds from the kitchen were reassuring. The men were still engrossed in their game and from the cheerful humor in his tones, Gus appeared to be winning.

Ted stared, fascinated, at the big, flat box before him. Common sense told him it was probably empty, or filled with worthless trash, but he couldn't help wondering if there might be money or jewels inside. If only he had a flashlight, or even a candle end, perhaps it would shine on gold coins or glittering stones! But there was not so much as a single match in his pockets.

He listened again to make sure he would not be disturbed, then drew a deep breath and pressed upward on the heavy lid. It moved with a faint snapping and groaning of rusty hinges. Little by little he raised it a foot and found that it could go no higher without striking the under side of a stair tread. But at last there was ample room for him to thrust an arm inside. All his hand encountered was a flat, smooth surface that felt like paper. Groping toward the side, he found a space where he could reach downward with his fingers and touch the edges of more big sheets of paper—hundreds of them, extending all the way to the bottom of the box.

Ted's mouth twisted in a wry grin. It served him right he thought—for getting all steamed up about finding treasure. It seemed like a queer thing, though, to lock up a lot of sheets of paper in a specially-built wooden chest. There must be something printed on them, but it was too dark to see.

Fumbling around behind him, the boy found the iron grenadier and set it under the box cover for a prop. Then with both hands he lifted out the heavy sheet that lay on top of the pile and crept back toward the door. When there was light enough he laid the huge paper flat on the floor and knelt above it.

Even in the dust and gloom of the closet, the words fairly leaped at him:

The

BIRDS OF AMERICA

from

ORIGINAL DRAWINGS

by

JOHN JAMES AUDUBON

Several lines of script lettering followed, listing the author's various honors and fellowships in learned societies. And still farther down the page were the words:

LONDON
Published by the Author
1827-38

Ted's lips pursed in a silent whistle and his eyes almost popped from their sockets. He stared at the beautifully engraved scrollwork around the old lettering, read the title once more, and crawled back to the box in silent haste.

In a moment he brought several more sheets forward to the light. The first one was blank, but as he uncovered the next he saw a picture that fairly took his breath away. It was a lordly turkey gobbler, almost life size, the bronze sheen of its feathers caught in brilliant color on the page. Below it he read the words: "I. Great American Cock, Meleagris Gallopavo, Male. Vulgo Wild Turkey."

The Latin meant little to Ted, but there was no question about its being a wild turkey. He feasted his eyes on the giant bird for a full minute before looking at the sheets that followed. The next hour was one of the most thrilling in the boy's life. He forgot all about the unfound treasure, and even the danger he was in, as he turned page after page. Many of the birds pictured were strange to him, but occasionally he came on an old friend—the Baltimore Oriole—the Song Sparrow—the Goldfinch—the Ruffed Grouse.

He tried not to leave thumb prints on any of the sheets he touched, for they were in beautiful condition. The tight, sturdy box had protected them from dust and dampness, and the fine rag paper had not yellowed with age.

It was the crash of a chair being overturned in the kitchen that brought him back to realities. Gus was cursing his luck. The game must have gone against him and soured his temper, for he continued to swear and fume for some moments. Carefully Ted laid the bird pictures and the title page back in the chest and eased the cover down. When he had locked it he put the key in his pocket once more and sprinkled dust over the wood to hide his finger marks. Then he closed the door of the closet and sat in the dark, listening.

Beyond the partition the big, shock-headed man kept up his tirade until he ran out of foul words. Then Ted heard him go lumbering over to the sink and pump himself a drink of water.

"I'm hungry again," he growled. "This lousy grub don't stay by you. What I want is a platter o' ham an' eggs."

A moment later he seemed to be rummaging in the cupboard where the canned goods were stored. "Say!" he exclaimed irritably. "You think it's funny, hidin' that peanut butter?"

Jake snorted. "You're der vun put it avay," he replied. "I tol' you it aind't dere."

"Somethin' mighty fishy about the whole thing," Gus muttered. "Jar was more'n half full when I cleaned up after breakfast. I'd ha' bet a dollar I put it right there next to the can o' peaches. But it's gone now, sure as shootin'. Well, I guess we got to eat plain bread from now on."

There was a clatter as he kicked the bread box

open, and then more grumbling.

"Even the bread's runnin' low," said Gus. "We can't stay here more'n another day or we'll starve to death."

"Bah!" Jake answered scornfully. "In der old country ve go t'ree—four days mit no food. Und all der time marching und fighting, ya!"

"Well, this ain't the old country," said Gus. "An' I'm used to gettin' my vittles reg'lar."

Ted heard him chewing a piece of bread noisily, then there was a sound of cans being opened and one of the men lighted the gasoline stove. They must be getting their noonday meal. After a few minutes the smell of hot coffee came stealing through the house and the boy pulled the belt of his jeans a notch tighter, trying to forget his own ravenous appetite.

He dozed for a while and when he woke the two men were playing pinochle again. The game went on and on. At length he heard a creak of boards as one of them got to his feet. "I'm sick o' this," came Gus's voice. "Let's go fishin'."

They took their time about leaving the house but he finally heard them go out the back door. When they had had time to get down to the creek bank he left his hiding place, pushing the door shut after him, and stole toward the kitchen. This time he meant to get away.

It was hard to leave the beautiful Audubon pictures, but the box was far too big and heavy for him to carry. Anyway, he was sure it would still be there when he returned. And he'd have Bill Gates and a squad of soldiers with him then!

The jar of peanut butter was in his hand as he tiptoed through the pantry. He looked around for a good place to leave it and finally decided to tuck it under the pillow on one of the cots. There was no way of knowing whose bed he had chosen, but he had to chuckle when he thought of the wranglings and accusations that would follow its discovery.

After a quick drink from the water pitcher, Ted reconnoitered the clearing through one of the rear windows and made sure the enemy was out of sight. Then he slipped out the door and darted into the underbrush. He went as quietly as he could, but the twigs and brambles caught at his clothes and in the dense thickets it was hard to see where he placed his feet. Once or twice dry sticks snapped under his feet and he crouched, listening, until he was sure he had not been heard.

He passed the big lilac bush and came to the corduroy road leading down into the swamp. This time there was nothing forbidding about the dark track through the cedars. Ted hurried along it at a trot, feeling less need for caution now that he was so far from the house. Soon he was moving along the ridge, with the tall cone of the ruined furnace looming on his left. He was out of breath now, but the taste of freedom was in his mouth and he ran even faster as he neared the place where he had pulled up the canoe.

It was still there, hidden in the blueberry bushes. Panting, he lifted the light craft by the gunwale and slipped its bow into the water. He picked up the paddle, shoved the canoe down the little beach and stepped in just as it floated free. Two or three quick strokes shot him forward into the narrow creek channel. And at that moment a rowboat came past a cedar clump, right across his bows. Before he could check the motion of the canoe it bumped lightly along the side of the boat. For an endless second the two men in the other craft stared at him, speechless with surprise. Then the squat, black-haired man who had been rowing reached out a huge paw and grasped the bow of the canoe.

"You move vunce," he growled, "und ve kill you!"

16

TED WAS TOO SHOCKED AND STAR-
tled to make a move if he had wanted to. After-
ward, when he thought about it, he knew he might
have plunged overboard and reached shore before
the men in the boat caught him. But at that moment all the strength seemed to ooze out of his arms
and legs and he sat as if paralyzed.

He recognized the big blond fellow sitting in
the stern. That was Gus. But it was the other man
whose eyes held his. They were a strange, pale gray,

cold as ice under the bristling, black brows. Somehow the boy had pictured Jake as a stolid, easy-going Dutchman, and he was wholly unprepared for such a face as this.

Suddenly Jake bowed his wide shoulders and shot a gorilla-like arm along the gunwale of the canoe. The next instant he had gripped Ted by the wrist and jerked him across into the boat.

"Vere you come from, huh?" he asked harshly, and when the boy made no answer, he gave his wrist an extra twist.

"N-no place," Ted choked. "I just—paddled down the creek for—for fun."

"You live near here?" Gus put in.

"Not very near. Up towards Mount Misery."

"Hm. What we goin' to do with him, Jake?"

The black-haired man scowled and picked up the oars. "Ve take him back to der house and ask some t'ings," he said. "Catch hold of der canoe."

Ted lay in the bottom of the boat between the feet of the two spies. Beside him on the planking was an eighteen-inch pickerel, still wriggling with life. It was funny, he thought, that he could look with interest at a fish when he was in such a predicament himself. But when it came to planning a way out, his usually quick mind was numb. All he could do was to face the blank fact of capture. He had ample proof that these were desperate men, careless of other people's lives, and if they knew what he had overheard they would hardly hesitate to do away with him.

But did they know? Neither of them had ever set eyes on him before. If he could keep up his pose of a luckless Piney who had strayed into their secret world, he might have a chance.

Jake pulled with quick, strong strokes, his baleful eyes fixed on Ted's face. Nobody spoke. Only the soft click of well-greased oarlocks broke the heavy silence of the swamp. The boat threaded a winding channel where the cedar shadows lay dark on the water and Jake turned the bow in toward the bank.

The landing place was cleverly concealed by low-hanging vines. Gus got out first, holding Ted by the arm, and they stood there while Jake pulled the boat and the canoe up on shore. Then, still in silence, they marched up the path to the house. Inside the kitchen, Jake moved a chair over with its back against the closed door and sat down.

" 'Fore we start in on him," said Gus, "I'd better search him. Looks like he's got somethin' there inside his shirt."

The man's huge hand ripped the buttons open and exposed the little green book. "Huh!" he exclaimed. "It's all about birds."

He thumbed over the pages and came to the front fly-leaf. "W. H. Gates," he read. "Is that what you're called?"

Ted swallowed hard. He wondered if the men had ever heard the name of their arch enemy. "No," he answered. "I'm Ted Winslow. Mr. Gates loaned me the book. He's—he's my teacher."

Gus handed the book over to his confederate and sat down where he, too, could see the boy's face. "Now, then," he began, "it's no use lyin' to us—"

"Shut up," said Jake coldly. "I ask him der qvestions. You—" he pointed a hairy forefinger at Ted's chest—"vas you effer here before?"

"No," Ted gulped. "I was just—"

"Vait! You didn' come to der house here?"

The boy shook his head desperately. "I tell you I never was around this swamp before in my life. I didn't even know there was a house—or anything."

Jake's pale eyes gave no hint as to whether the statement was believed. His stare continued to bore through Ted until the boy squirmed. "Vat time you leaf home?" his inquisitor went on.

"About seven o'clock, I guess—I haven't got a watch—"

"Today?"

Ted couldn't speak. He nodded miserably, hoping the untruth would be forgiven him.

"He's lyin'," Gus put in. "You go ahead an' work on him. I'll get that fish cleaned for supper."

Jake got up as the other man went out. He reached in one of his pockets and pulled forth a neatly coiled length of heavy twine. "Turn aroundt," he growled.

Ted felt his arms gripped behind him and in an

instant the cord was biting into his crossed wrists. When they were tightly bound, Jake pushed him across the room and passed the free end of the cord over a stout peg, high in the wall. Then he pulled down on it till the boy's hands were lifted high behind him and he stood on tiptoe, panting with pain.

Jake moved a chair over and sat down, still holding the end of the cord. His cruel lips were twisted into a grin. "Pretty soon," he said, "maybe you talk, ya? Ve find out somet'ings."

Ted gritted his teeth, fiercely determined that he would say no more. Two or three agonizing minutes dragged by and the black-haired alien reached forward leisurely to pull up another notch on the cord. Ted's aching arms felt as if they would be wrenched out of their sockets, but he only set his jaw tighter and strained upward on his toes. He lost track of time and concentrated on enduring from one moment to the next. If he could get his mind off his torture he thought it might help. In brief intervals between the twinges of pain he tried to picture what might be happening at home.

When he failed to return last night at milking time, Grandpa Winslow must have begun to worry. By morning he'd have gone to Joe Lucas or one of the other neighbors and tried to get up a search party. But where would they hunt for him? Bitterly he blamed himself for keeping his plan a secret. He'd wanted to show off—prove how smart he was and surprise everybody! But if no Piney but old Cudjaw Tewks had discovered this place in a hundred years, what chance was there of their finding him now?

Bill Gates offered the one glimmer of hope. If his grandfather told the lieutenant about his disappearance, Gates might remember their talks about Hoquadunk Creek and the Lost Forge. They'd have to bring boats, though, and if they started from the place where Bill had found the provisions there was no telling how long they would have to explore before they reached the island.

The cord on his wrists was raised another notch and a groan of suffering came from between Ted's clenched teeth. He knew he couldn't stand much more. His knees were trembling now, and if they gave way his whole weight would be hanging from his wrists.

At that moment the door swung open and Gus came in with the cleaned pickerel in his hand. He gave an evil chuckle at the sight of the white-faced boy. "Makin' him do a little dance, eh?" he said. "That'll learn him to keep his nose out of other folks' business."

He rinsed his hands under the pump and slouched over to one of the cots. As he stretched himself out to enjoy the spectacle his head bumped something hard under the pillow.

"What the—" he growled. "Oh, so that's where you stuck it. Bein' funny again, were you, Jake?"

He held up the peanut butter jar and shot a sour look at his partner.

Jake frowned. "Giff it to me," he snapped. "Dot's it! Der boy vas here. Look—dere iss more gone."

He threw a double half hitch in the twine to hold it in place and strode across to the cot, pointing a triumphant finger at the level of the peanut butter in the glass.

"You mean you didn't put it under the pillow?" Gus asked. There was a puzzled look on his stupid face. "Well, for gosh sakes! He must ha' been here in the house this mornin' before breakfast. But how'd he git in while we was both right here?"

"Dumkopf!" Jake snarled. "He vas in der house all night!"

The words rang with a terrifying sound in Ted's ears. After them there was only roaring blackness. His knees sagged, the cord broke, and he slumped in an unconscious heap on the floor.

A sudden splash of cold water in his face brought the tortured boy back from oblivion. For an instant he could not remember where he was or what had happened. Then the sickening truth was all too clear, as he stared up into the ugly faces above him.

"Listen, you," Gus threatened. "We'll paste the livin' daylights out o' you, if you don't spill it now. What time did you come here yesterday?"

"In the afternoon," Ted answered weakly. "I

didn't know there was anybody here."

"Where'd you go when we come in?"

The boy gestured toward the pantry door. "Back in there," he said.

"Come on—git up. You got to show us."

Ted struggled to his knees and Jake hauled him erect with a rough hand. He staggered dizzily as he led the way through the pantry and the dining-room. "I hid in the hall," he told them.

"Vait! I see der tracks," Jake exclaimed. He followed the blurred footprints in the dust, bending low to see better in the dim light. At the stairs he hesitated, casting about like a hound on a scent, then picked up the trail again. It led through the narrow passage beside the staircase and straight back to the closet hiding-place.

"Diss iss it," the black-haired man muttered, opening the door. He pointed to some scattered crumbs of bread on the floor. Then he crawled into the opening and rapped his knuckles on the partition.

"Take him back in der kitchen, Gus," he ordered.

"Say somet'ings like you vas chust talking."

Gus pushed the groggy youngster ahead of him through the rooms. When they reached the kitchen he motioned to the boy to sit down and began to speak in a low voice.

"If he can hear what I'm sayin'," he told Ted, "then it might be you know too much for your health. Were you listenin' to us last night?"

The boy gulped. "I—I could hear voices," he stammered. "It sounded as if you were playing cards or something."

Gus nodded grimly. "What else?" he asked.

"Nothing—except I could hear you cooking supper, and—and washing the dishes."

Jake came swiftly back to the kitchen. When he entered, his face was like a thundercloud. "Dot's enough," he said. "I could hear every vord. Cook der fish, Gus, und ve get oudt. But first I make sure he aind't ever tell not'ings."

He gripped the terrified boy by the nape of the neck and pushed him toward the back door. But Gus was there before them. Moving his big bulk with surprising speed, he blocked the exit.

"Hold on, Jake," he said. "I don't want no trouble with you, but there's no call to murder the kid in cold blood. He's nothin' but a harmless Piney. Chances are he didn't know what we was talkin' about, an' wouldn't remember if he did."

"Ach, you fool!" the black-haired man snarled. "You vant to be caught, huh? Not me! Und I giff der orders here."

Gus stood like a rock. "You ain't givin' this one," he said, and there was a hard glint in his eyes. "I reckon I'm as tough as any o' you heinies, an' I've earned my pay doin' your dirty work. But I didn't contract for this sort o' thing. Use your head, Jake. Nobody's goin' to find the boy very soon if we leave him tied up here. His folks would ha' been here 'fore this if they knew where he was. All we need's a night's start."

Jake seemed to hesitate. Ted felt the fingers holding his neck relax slowly. Then he was thrown out of the way with such sudden violence that he fell headlong to the floor. There was a quick shuffle of

258

feet behind him and a crash that shook the old house. He looked up in time to see Jake roll over like a cat and come up on his toes, a long knife glinting in his hand. Gus must have knocked him down with a blow of his fist. On the foreigner's bloody face there was such a look of hate as the boy had never seen, and cold murder glared from his pale eyes.

Gus crouched a little, his back still to the door, his big fists hanging loosely at his sides. As the black-haired man advanced toward him he shifted his weight, rocking forward and back on pillar-like legs. Then Jake darted in with the vicious suddenness of a striking snake. Ted saw the knife flash and at the same instant Gus balanced against the door frame and swung a huge foot into his opponent's midriff.

The breath went out of Jake with a sound like a locomotive exhaust—*hooh!* And while he still writhed on the floor, Gus picked up a chair and smashed him over the head with it. That ended the fight. The black-haired alien was either dead or unconscious.

For a moment Gus stood over him with the broken chair in his hand, waiting to make sure he was not shamming. Then he swung on Ted. "Turn over, you," he panted. "Just because I didn't let him drownd you, it's no sign you're goin' loose."

He picked up the long end of the cord that still bound the boy's wrists behind him and tied it tightly to his ankles, jerking them up till a scant six inches of taut line separated his hands and feet.

"There," he said. "It'll take you a while to get out o' that. An' I'll just bust a hole in your canoe so you won't be leavin' here too quick."

He recovered Jake's knife from the floor and tossed it out the door into the thick brush. Then methodically he moved around the kitchen, preparing a meal. He filled the coffee-pot, lighted the stove and set about frying the pickerel.

Ted lay on his side, bearing as best he could the pain of the cord that cut into his chafed wrists. In spite of his discomfort, he felt a kind of drowsy peace. He had been too close to death to mind the mere fact of being bound. How he would get free was a problem he would have to face later, but now there was nothing to do but lie still and sniff the pleasant aroma of the cooking fish.

Gus jerked a sheet off one of the cots and took it into the dining-room. When he returned he was carrying the cloth by the corners like a sack and it was heavy with the old silver he had hastily gathered. The burden made a musical, clinking sound when he laid it down.

He flipped the well-browned pickerel over with a fork and turned off the stove. Getting bread from the box and opening the peanut butter jar, he began to wolf down his meal. Once he stopped in the midst of a big mouthful and cut off the tail end of the fish.

"Here," he mumbled, dropping the piece of fish on a plate along with a slice of dry bread. "You ain't likely to get much to eat for a while." And he shoved the plate close to Ted's face.

Tied up as he was, the boy was in too much bodily pain to have a great deal of appetite left, and he lay motionless, making no effort to reach the plate.

Gus scowled at him. "Now listen, punk," he said. "Nobody refuses vittles that I offer 'em, an' that's a perfectly good piece o' fish. You saw what I done to my friend, there. If I was you I'd get busy right quick an' show some politeness."

He grinned as the boy strained forward, trying to bite the food with his teeth, but he made no move to help him. "That'll give you somethin' to do," he said.

When the big man had finished eating he wiped his fingers on his trousers and went over to the prostrate Jake. "Get up," he growled, stirring the huddled figure with his boot toe. "A tough guy like you ain't goin' to be laid out long by a little clout on the skull. There's a long way to go, an' I don't aim to have to carry you."

As there was no response, Gus pumped a pitcher full of water at the sink and soused it over the other man's head.

Jake stirred weakly and a moan came from his battered lips. "Come on," urged Gus, "we got to be travelin'."

He was stooping down to lift the heavy body when there was a sound of movement outside. At the same instant a voice Ted knew spoke from the doorway. "Just let him lie there, and you—stand up. Get your hands over your head!"

17

FROM WHERE TED LAY IT WAS IMPOSsible to get a view of the man at the door. But he could see Gus slowly straighten up, lifting his empty hands high above him.

"All right, Corporal," the familiar voice ordered, "tie him up. Make sure first that he isn't armed. And you'd better have a couple of men take care of that fellow on the floor. He acts as if he's getting ready to come to. I'll go look for the boy."

There was a clumping of thick-soled infantry

shoes at the entrance and several men came into the room. Ted squirmed around until he could see them. He tried to shout aloud, but all his voice produced was a tired squeak.

"Hey—Bill Gates! Here I am, back o' the table!"

The lieutenant had sharp ears. He turned quickly, but in the fading light of late afternoon he had difficulty in seeing the boy's huddled form for a moment.

"Ted?" he asked. "Oh, there you are! Well for Pete's sake, son—they've got you hog-tied for fair!"

Grinning, he bent above him and whipped out a pocket-knife to cut his bonds. Then the grin turned into an angry frown. "Holy smokes," he growled, "look at those wrists! I ought to have shot that guy!"

Ted sat up, pulling his cramped arms forward painfully. The wrists were puffy and bleeding, where the thin cord had cut into them, but he was so overjoyed at his rescue that he no longer minded.

"Gee, Bill," he choked, "I never was so glad to see anybody in all my life. You got here just in time, too. They'd have skipped out in another ten minutes."

"That one with the busted head doesn't look as if he'd have done much skipping," said the lieutenant. "What happened to him, anyway?"

"Oh, that was just from a row they had about whether to drown me or leave me tied up here. I reckon Jake isn't really hurt. He's too tough."

Gates lifted the boy up and set him on the nearest cot. "You rest a bit till the stiffness goes out of your legs," he said. "How'd you like something to eat?"

"Boy!" Ted breathed. "I could sure go for some real food. Gus gave me a piece o' fish, but I had trouble getting at it with my hands tied."

"I expected you might be hungry," the lieutenant told him. "So I brought along some grub in a package. Here, try a cheese sandwich."

Ted took a good-sized bite and chewed happily. "How'd you ever know where to hunt for me?" he asked.

For answer, Gates went quickly to the door and

whistled. "Let him loose," he called to somebody outside. And an instant later Ted heard a scrabble of claws on the steps. Into the room came Tramp like a black whirlwind.

The dog sniffed once, cocking his head as he surveyed the crowded kitchen, then hurled himself at his master in a frenzy of delight. Ted had a struggle to keep from being smothered by his moist caresses.

"We used him for a bloodhound," Gates chuckled as he came back to the cot. "Soon as we knew you'd borrowed Lucas' canoe the rest was easy. I had a hunch you might have come down this way, so we put a boat on the truck and started, with Tramp riding beside me. When we came down the highway to that culvert over the stream he wanted to get out. So we launched the boat there and let him lead us along the bank."

"Gee!" said Ted, fondling the big dog's head. "But I sent him home when I was way up the creek. He didn't know the rest of the way."

"He must have followed you along shore. Anyhow, he brought us opposite the upper island where you landed the canoe. We found the mark of the keel in the sand. From there on it was fairly simple."

"Did you see the old furnace—and the piece of iron with Classon's name on it?" Ted put in. "Gee, did I get a kick out o' finding that!"

Gates nodded. "Yes, we came past the furnace and took a look. You had a right to be pleased. That's a real discovery, Ted, and I shouldn't wonder if you'd be famous, once the historical societies get wind of it."

He pointed to the bulky bundle tied up in the sheet, which still lay where Gus had dropped it. "What's in that?" he asked curiously.

"It's silver out o' the dining-room," said Ted. "Gus was all set to carry it off with him. This house is full of old things—all left just the way they were when folks lived here. What I can't see is why the owners didn't take the stuff with 'em. It must be valuable."

"Say, that *is* mighty strange," said Gates. "How are your legs by now? I think you and I ought to take a look around the house. Maybe we can solve the mystery."

"Shucks, I'm fine," Ted told him, and walked a few steps to prove it. "Come on—there's something special I want you to see."

The lieutenant gave his men orders to take the two prisoners outside and keep them under close guard. Then he opened the sheet and looked at the pile of silver. What he saw made him whistle.

"Some of these pieces are really beautiful," he said. "I don't know what they'd be worth as antiques, but it would be a lot of money. Let's see what else we can find."

He led the way into the dining-room and stood for a while admiring its fine proportions and heavy old furniture. Then he studied the portrait over the sideboard, brushing away some of the dust with his handkerchief.

"These people had taste as well as money," he said thoughtfully. "My guess is that some pretty well-known painter in New York or Philadelphia did this picture. It's more of a puzzle than ever,

Ted."

He moved on into the hall and crossed it to the locked door on the opposite side. When he put the weight of his shoulder against it, the bolt split the old wood and gave way. Together they entered a long, somber room with four vine-darkened windows opening on its northern side. Ranged formally along the wall there were spindly-legged chairs with tattered brocade upholstery, and two tall, tarnished mirrors hung at crazy angles above tiny side tables. The only other furniture was a dusty square piano of huge size standing in a corner.

"I'd call this the drawing-room," Gates mused. "They probably gave very elegant dances here once, though the poor old floor doesn't look much like it now."

Many of the window-panes were broken in this room, and the rain and snow of countless seasons had come in to warp and rot the boards. Treading carefully, Gates went over to the piano and lifted the mahogany lid to disclose ivory keys, yellowed with age and neglect. He touched one or two and a discordant jangling came from the vitals of the old instrument. Then, peering more closely at the name of the maker on the under side of the lid, he pointed to the date—1827.

"That doesn't tell us much," he frowned, "except that somebody lived here a long time after Jared Classon first bought the iron works land. Come on upstairs. I've got to find out what happened or I won't be able to sleep tonight."

As they passed through the hall, Ted started to tell his friend about the special discovery he had made in the hall closet, but he checked himself, knowing that could wait. The contagion of the search had caught him now and he was as eager as Gates to get to the bottom of the mystery.

It was nearly dark now. The lieutenant switched on a flashlight to guide their steps up the treacherous stairway. At the curved landing, halfway up, they had to climb over a tangled barrier of debris, but they reached the second floor without mishap.

There were four big bedrooms opening off the upper hall. In two of them they found the beds neatly made and all the furnishings in order, although huge cobwebs hung from the ceilings and mice and squirrels had made nests in the blankets and mattresses.

The third chamber they entered showed evidences of more disorder. The bedding had been left in a tumbled heap at the foot of the big four-poster. From the old bottles, brushes and other toilet articles on the dressing table, it appeared that this had been a woman's room.

Bill Gates pulled open drawers and rummaged through closets with military thoroughness. He fingered the frail silk of dresses and negligees, and shook his head. "No woman would ever willingly go off and leave these things," he growled impatiently. "It sure beats me!"

There was one more room to explore. The door was closed and locked and the husky soldier had to use all his strength to force it. Inside, the beam of the flashlight showed them two beds, one large and the other smaller—a child's cot. Here again the bedclothes were disheveled. A pair of trousers of old-fashioned cut lay in a rumpled heap across a chair. In addition to the big bureau and other bedroom furniture there was a tall mahogany secretary against the farther wall.

Gates went straight across to it. "If the answer's anywhere, it's here," he said, and turned the brass key in the slanting lid.

As it creaked open, Ted saw a litter of documents and letters, strewn on the desk top, and bulging from pigeonholes. Gates gave him the light to hold and ruffled through the papers with practiced hands.

"Bills, receipts, lists of iron shipments," he muttered. "Mostly business papers. But somewhere he must have—wait! Here it is!"

His fingers pounced on a small, leather-bound book, tucked away in one of the pigeonholes.

"It's a sort of journal," Gates said, leafing quickly through it. "Seems to cover about six years, starting in 1835. Let's see what these last few pages say."

He flattened the little book so that Ted could read with him. The ink had faded to a brownish gray, but the writing was so even and clear that the words were easily legible.

"November 9, 1841," the boy read. "A white frost this morning, the first of the year. The last heat was drawn from the furnace yesterday. I fear it may be some time before we fire again, for the Pennsylvania furnaces are underselling any price we can make. All of the burners and iron workers have been discharged excepting my foreman, Ames. One of the servants, Dinah, came down sick last night and seems in great pain. Shot four ducks today."

The next entry was dated four days later. "Our poor cook Dinah died this day, and her daughter, Cindy, is now sick of the same illness. Though I have kept it from my wife I am troubled that the disease is small pox! Yesterday I sent Ames on a good horse for the doctor, but he has not yet returned. I buried Dinah, with Cato's help, and burned her clothing. God protect us all if this is what I fear.

"November 17, 1841. That scoundrel Ames has taken French leave. It must be he suspected the plague, for we have seen nothing of him or of the doctor. Cindy died today and Cato is very ill. My poor Angelina is so much afeared that she will not let me stir from the house. She keeps little Jonathan shut in above stairs so that he may be clear of the infection, but without servants she must cook the meals and nurse Cato herself. We have burned sulphur in the servants' quarters and there is little more to do but trust in our Creator."

There was only one more entry, hastily scrawled under the date of November 24th.

"I am leaving this house that has meant all my life to me. This day my wife died in great suffering. I have dug her grave and will bury her beside the lilac bush she planted. After Cato's death we burned the servants' house, but it was too late to save my beloved Angelina . . ."

The next few words were blotted. Then ". . . take my son Jonathan with me and try to reach Pemberton tonight. There is a doctor there. The child is ill of a fever. It has begun to snow and a storm is rising."

That was all. Gates looked at Ted and closed the

book reverently.

"Poor devil," he said. "He never got through to Pemberton. The chances are he and his little boy were lost in the blizzard. That would explain it all, for you can bet Ames would never tell what happened. He'd be lynched if he did. Come on, youngster, this place makes me blue."

Ted had a choky feeling himself as he went down the stairs. "I—I reckon I found a pair o' Jonathan's skates," he said. "They were in this closet back here. An' there's something else I want to show you if you'll bring the light."

One by one, the boy fished the various articles out of the closet and laid them in a pile. At last he was able to get hold of the corners of the flat box and drag it forward into the little circle of light.

Before he lifted the cover he turned to Gates with a worried expression on his face. "I don't know who all this stuff belongs to," he said, "but do you s'pose I could keep this one thing for myself?"

The lieutenant smiled. "The law will probably decide if there are any heirs," he said. "But I should think you might lay claim to at least one thing, as long as you did the discovering. What is it—a croquet set?"

Ted raised the cover and the light from the flash fell on the beautifully engraved lettering of the Audubon title page.

Gates took a quick step forward. "Great Scott!" he murmured under his breath. "The Elephant Folio!"

"No," said Ted, "there's no elephants in it. It's about birds!"

"I'll say it is! The greatest bird book that ever was made—but this first edition is called the Elephant Folio because it's so big! And in perfect condition, too. Holy cats, Ted—what a find!"

"You mean there aren't many like this?"

Gates lifted page after page and feasted his eyes on the warm color of the engravings. Then he laid them back as tenderly as if they had been made of spun glass.

"What's that?" he said. "Many like this? My boy, there were less than two hundred sets printed.

They're rarer than dodo's eggs. The last one I heard about was sold for twelve thousand dollars—and it was nowhere near as fine a set as this!"

"Gosh!" Ted breathed in awe. "I guess I couldn't have it, then."

"You're darn right you'll have it, if I have anything to say about it," said the lieutenant vehemently. "Ted, there's a college education and just about anything else you want, in that box. And you've sure earned it, this last week. Now that we've got this spy ring rounded up, I'm going to see that you have a special citation from the War Department. A boy with your spunk is worth as much to the country as a first-class soldier."

"Gee!" said Ted. "I didn't do so much. An' I clean forgot to tell you that I heard where the spies' headquarters are in New York! That's why Jake strung me up by the wrists—to make me tell how much I knew."

He repeated the instructions that Jake had given Gus.

"Man—that sounds like the real thing!" Gates

beamed. "I'll get a message to headquarters as soon as we're back, and that place'll be raided tomorrow."

He looked at his wrist watch. "Six o'clock. We'd better hustle, or it'll soon be too dark to follow the creek."

"Oh, well," the boy replied, "we've still got Tramp to show us!"

They carried the big box out and two of the soldiers took it carefully down to the flat-bottomed boat in which they had come. In the gathering dusk Ted stood for a moment looking back at the dark old house before he and his dog got into the canoe.

The place no longer made him feel lonesome or sad, now that he knew its history. There had been love and kindness there as well as tragedy. And the evil men who had used it in these recent days had left no lasting mark upon it. Now that the shadow was gone from the Pines, it would be fun to bring Grandpa Winslow down here and let him see that there was a real "Lost Forge."

Thinking of his grandfather made him remember it was chore-time. "Gosh!" he said, as he scrambled into the canoe. "Come on, Tramp—we'll be late for the milking again!"

And digging deep with his paddle he set out in the wake of Bill Gates' boat, headed for home.

THE END

ATLANTIC
Barnegat
Tom's River
Forked River
Rt. 40
Lakehurst Naval Station
Old Road
P L
Fort Dix
Creature Comfort
Mt. Misery
Fire Tower
Lebanon State Forest
New
Philadelphia
N
E
S
W

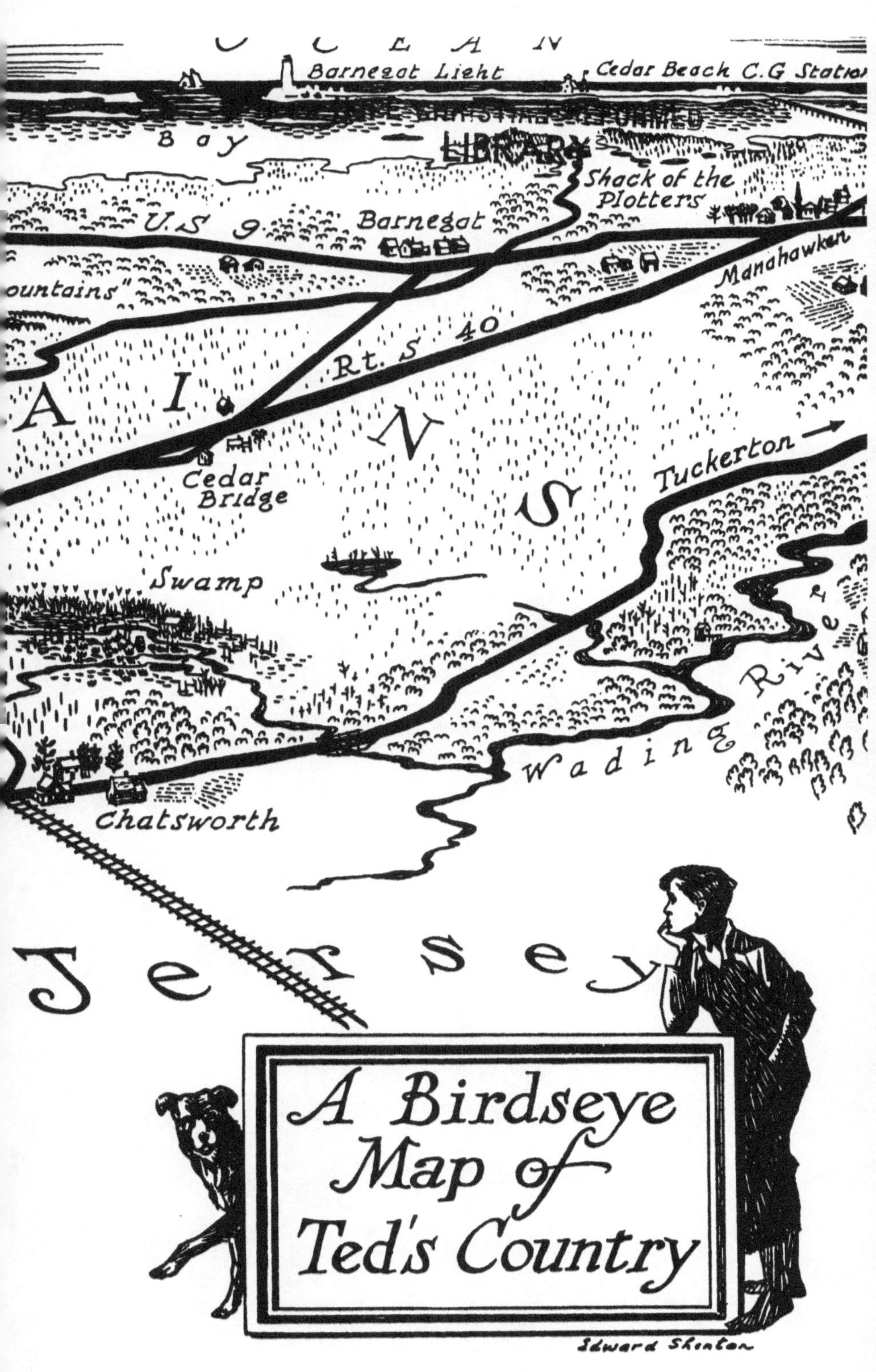

O C E A N
Barnegat Light
Cedar Beach C.G. Station
Bay
Barnegat
Shack of the Plotters
U S 9
Manahawken
ountains"
Rt. S 40
A I N S
Cedar Bridge
Tuckerton
Swamp
Wading River
Chatsworth
Je r s e y
A Birdseye Map of Ted's Country
Edward Shenton